OUT OF SHADOW FOREST

A FANTASY NOVEL

SWORD MASTER OF HONEY HEART RESORT

JONATHAN EVAN HUDSON

OUT OF SHADOW FOREST

CHAPTER I

ROMEO

R omeo Bladell knew, for sure he knew, that there were absolutely no roosters in the middle of Shadow Forest, and yet that cock-a-doodle-do was no doubt so very rooster-like, wow. It was as loud and proud as any rooster challenging the sun in the morning, a mere bird that was determined to rise higher and brighter than the sun itself.

His back was to a wide mossy trunk of another oak, while he sat knees to chest on an incredibly thick and low winding branch, all hiding among the countless broad leaves.

Alone this time, for now, but the murk around him was more than bright enough for the morning. Plenty of light was sprinkled everywhere like the many, many crumbs of Aunt Tilda's famously delicious peach pies for dessert.

She even insisted that without the countless crumbs it just wouldn't be peach pie.

Just like without sprinkles of sunlight, it just wouldn't be a proper morning in Shadow Forest … kinda.

What Romeo would do for a taste of one of Aunt Tilda's peach pies right now … but she'd smack him silly for yearning for a dessert when it was time for breakfast. Bad enough that cock-a-doodle-do was getting louder and louder.

Closer and closer.

Don't think of a good greasy eggs and bacon breakfast right now. The kind of breakfast both his ma and Aunt Tilda were famous for.

But no doubt the source of the cock-a-doodle-do was on the ground. A good several paces below the very branch Romeo slept on. Every inch and cranny of his body ached but, like pa often said, that was just another way his body let him know he was still very much alive and well, despite whatever beating he took earlier, or, in this case, his makeshift bed helped him survive another night in Shadow Forest and its countless horrors within its endless murk.

That he slept in his red jerkin and brown slacks, sigh. If only he hadn't skipped the shirt so many days ago, but no crying over spilt milk.

Even better, Aunt Tilda wasn't here to wallop him either, for daring to think about spilling some precious milk again.

But ack!

Twigs snapped loud and clear nearby, but behind him. Leaves rustled. Crackled. Ferns got scrapped. The source coming his direction, from behind, and it sounded like it was far bigger than any rooster.

Closer to the size of a wolf.

Maybe bigger.

Thankfully Velvet Ruins let him hold onto one of her precious scimitars. Its curved blade was a wicked lightning violet and yet there was no doubt it was forged from human bone. The lavender handle felt like quality ivory too, but they both knew it was somehow forged from human remains, at least from what Velvet was told. The balance was so perfect, so solid, but not too heavy, not too light, he was still utterly shocked at the scimitar's quality.

Nothing short of the best for a clawgirl like Velvet Ruins.

Well, before clawgirls like her got demoted to fodder slaved to their lessers. Lessers clawgirls used to command themselves.

A fate Romeo saved Velvet from.

Back a few days ago she showed her appreciation by not just fighting beside him, but fighting with him in the gorgeously bare utterly nude to as the sexiest thank you ever.

Well, recently, when his other clawgirl girlfriends insisted Velvet finally let her outfit regenerate from his Puributcher Technique and, ugh, that no-sex-until-safe policy hammered away another joy in life.

But in return Velvet got to guard Romeo for the last few days, and with her velvety voice, she was one fine singer, singing him gently to sleep each and every night.

A cool breeze stirred through the forest, rustling countless leaves, and right into his broad but now scruffy face. It filled his breath with the natural musty earthiness of these woods, and best of all, that strangely natural almond and vanilla musk of the stunningly gorgeous Velvet, who, was hidden by a strategic cluster of broad leaves from all directions except his own.

She was laying down a pace ahead of him, and still snoozing sexy on the very same branch, but unfortunately, now fully dressed. Her violet leotard fit perfectly, with pink hearts in choice places to emphasize her lushest curves.

As in curved perfectly slim in the right spots, and super-heavy in the moneymaking chest spots.

Just like how her fine smooth skin had such an exotically tanned complexion like toasted almonds and was just as sweet on the eyes. While her gorgeous heart of a baby face was framed with long lush black hair that went curly at the bottom, near her shoulder blades, even after she slept sexy sweet for him on her side. Also so that her other scimitar laid above her, strapped to her side facing the sky, easily in reach.

She slept over a nice thick patch of moss, even if she deserved far more than that extra comfort, and not just from all the sexy she offered him these last few days.

Especially after saving him time and time again from hazards he himself missed, to, no doubt, the chagrin of pa and his grandpa.

But while her bright beautifully violet eyes met his, clearly wide and worried, her cherry-lipped grimace was directed downward ... and—

Another cock-a-doodle-do?

Velvet shuttered, eyes shutting. Shivering.

Cringing?

Romeo gasped. Tried to catch her attention again. Ask

what was wrong without speaking the words and revealing their location.

But no.

Velvet started to curl up. As if ... if the very sound of the rooster was hurting her?

And hurting her badly.

CHAPTER 2
ROMEO

No. It couldn't be a rooster.

The rustles below, of leaves being stepped on heavily, crinkling, and the scrapping of many ferns together, snapping more than a few of their stems along the way ... no.

It sounded like it was at least as big as a wolf. Maybe bigger.

No rooster was that big.

But then what was it? Romeo never heard of any legend about monsters with rooster-like calls. Or that clawgirls like Velvet had any dislike of roosters. No. Her kind were meant to be able to hide among mankind. Seduce and slay guys like Romeo, but not all clawgirls embraced such a vile lifestyle. More than a few didn't, actually, since a human's lifestyle nowadays, not so bad. It was so good that a number of the gorgeous girls working off their debts at the Honey Heart

Resort run by Aunt Tilda turned out to be clawgirls enjoying their human lifestyle, for the most part, at least.

There was no chance Velvet would be weak against an actual rooster or its call.

If only he could check on his other clawgirl girlfriends, but he wasn't about to leave Velvet here alone and vulnerable.

The twisting limbs full of big broad oak leaves around this winding thick branch hid Romeo from the creature, but also hid the creature form him.

Same for Velvet, who, only a pace away, was curled up like a fetal baby on the thick soft moss and trembling now.

Romeo had to move. To get up. His suede boots were more like suede socks. They'd let him feel the rough bark of the tree.

But that wouldn't stop the bark from crumbling, snapping underneath his movement.

And making a sound when Velvet was so vulnerable ... no. He gripped the ivory-like handle of this precious scimitar. Shifting around to seek a better view of the coming danger.

Wait.

Not a single songbird chirped. Not a single squirrel scampered. The forest was all but silent.

Even Velvet was utterly silent in her cringing pain.

Romeo gnashed his teeth—silently. That clinched it. The small forest critters knew this world better than he did.

Whatever was cock-a-doodling was a dangerous monster.

The branch Romeo and Velvet were on was at least several

paces above the creature, but no telling how high it could jump. If it was a bird-like monster, it might even be able to fly, some, or at least jump high and glide.

Even chickens could jump high and glide.

Well, some breeds of chicken. Especially certain roosters.

How many times had Romeo, back at home as a little young brat chased the chickens until the rooster came and defended them with its cocky proud life and even defeated him more often than not.

Partly because ma would smack him silly if he hurt the chickens too badly. Let along scare them too badly.

But this creature was no farm rooster. Ambush the monster or ... Velvet flicked her foot at him.

Shook her head at him.

Finger over mouth and silently hushed him.

Before cringing in utter agony once again.

He nodded. Hand tight on her scimitar.

When a chuckle ran out below. A very human but sinister chuckle.

And his blood run colder than ice.

CHAPTER 3
VIVIAN

Vivian gasped silently,, in utter, utter totallies pain at the sudden cock-a-doodle-do crackling and echoing through every nick and cranny of Shadow Forest.

Like a kick in the gut, every bit of the rooster's call kicked her more and more, and then throughout every bit of her body, her body forcing her to curl up, gasp silently more and more at the pain starring her vision blurry, enough to force her eyes were to squint through the crust from last night's sleep. A nightly sleep she had started to savor, since her duties at the Honey Heart Resort left little time for beauty sleep.

Yet now, Vivian cringed as tightly as her own awfully revealing leotard of pink with pale pink hearts clung to her. Her long naturally pink hair covered her, but couldn't hide her from the source of that agony.

The bed of thick soft moss she had slept on suddenly felt bumpier, more jagged than any of this oak's bark anywhere. Like bugs were crawling through the moss, up around her leotard, and into her bracers and even into her thigh boots.

Yet she cringed so tight, so awfully horrible, that she couldn't even rub herself, try to scrub those bugs off her.

Nothing but the cock-a-doodle-do reached her ears. Not even her own heart beat, the rooster was so loud.

But why?

How could a rooster do this to her? No.

It couldn't be rooster. This was Shadow Forest. She was a good few branches away from her dear Romeo. That cocky Velvet stole Vivian's place for the last few nights and and and ...

Shaking by her waist. Violent shaking.

And not by her?

Her sword?!

The Savage Sword of Shadow Forest!

A wicked scimitar in more ways than one. Its blade was like an evil deer antler curved drastically and sharpened worse than any blade she ever saw.

Even compared to Romeo's harpe, a beautifully crescent blade.

Last time she wielded this savage blade, dared touch its handle, the black hilt and dark red handle had swallowed her hands together into a painful spiky ball and ... this pain from the cock-a-doodle-do ...

Nothing compared to **that** pain.

That terror.

Vivian didn't dare moan, but she did reach for her lone but dangerous blade.

CHAPTER 4
ROMEO

Romeo held his breath throughout the entire chuckle. A very human chuckle several paces straight below him. Heavy footsteps crinkled dry leaves, snapping ferns sharply, and cracking hard leather sole against solid granite, the sounds all spoke of a solidly built man.

But this was Shadow Forest, so best not be too certain.

The thick winding branch Romeo was sitting on would only do some much to hide their presence from the man below. Even with the many clusters of broad oak leaves. The many off-shooting branches.

His jerkin was too bright a red.

Velvet had a leotard that was far too bright violet.

Both easily seen from below—at the right angle. A few to several paces beyond beneath the branch and looking up, and around.

No wonder the songbirds and squirrels were utterly

utterly silent. It was so silent his own heart pounded far too loudly in his ears, ready to beat the music of battle, but to fight another human, and without an obvious reason or direct threat ... not like he hadn't done so.

He saved Velvet by slaying some clawgirl hunters. Using his Slash-o-Boom technique. One technique of many of his sword techniques.

But not as an ambush. Romeo had tried talking them down. Just like pa would have done.

Still, maybe the guy below was another clawgirl hunter. That there were so many hunters out here, this deep in Shadow Forest ... strange.

Unless that monstrous necromancer who slaved Romeo's clawgirl girlfriends was sending them, somehow. Gold was an amazing motivator to the wrong sort of men. No question why. The necromancer could easily revive dead clawgirls and if the clawgirls were undead, there was no way for Romeo to save them except to end their miserable undead existence.

Velvet, even if she recovered enough to move from her mossy bed on the branch, she couldn't fight like this, and especially now that she only had one scimitar on her. Without both scimitars she couldn't snap the pommels together into a scimitar bow and fire any bolts from a distance.

Not right now.

No. This was all up to Romeo. Up to Romeo to save her, once again, and save her he would, somehow.

But announcing there position seemed ... far too foolish. Too foolish for words.

And yet an ambush—no. Pa would never approve.

No guarantee this man was even an enemy.

"You sure they're here, Grif?"

A growl and snort? Paces below Velvet.

And a hint of smoke. Of burning bird flesh?

Like Uncle Jethron always said, trust your nose.

"They're here. I smell 'em, Midus."

Oh no. Velvet had a lovely but potent almond and vanilla musk after all, so anyone with a decent nose could locate her easily. Romeo had to get these men and their rooster monster away from Velvet, but without leaving Velvet alone. Then he could try talking to them. Maybe.

"Which direction?" Midus said.

More deep breaths. Rasping. Dry.

"Up," Grif said, "In the tree."

Another chuckle. Romeo tightened his grip on the scimitar. No point hiding now.

"Come on." Midus said, "Come on, little clawgirls, or ..."

Another cock-a-doodle-do. From right below them? Loud enough to jab his ears and gut like pa getting another strike in on him during a bout.

But Velvet ... she cringed even more, curled tight even more.

Trembled in agony.

Romeo leapt up. Right by Velvet.

And bared the scimitar she gave him.

"Go away," Romeo said, "You're not wanted here."

Two chuckles now.

SWOOSH!

SMASH!

The branches and leaves hiding them vanished. In an instant.

Ripped away by a dark blur.

And revealed the horrors that had to be defeated—or else.

CHAPTER 5
KROTHA RIGOT

Krotha Rigot chuckled with bloodthirsty glee. The cold pitch dark surrounded her, just like the hole within her, deep within her head, making it both lighter and heavier, and filled with pure raging hatred as dark and deep as this unending abyss itself.

Just like her demon core, the hole within her.

A core reaching its final state of perfection.

The disgustingly bright rainbow of spider threads crowned the circular hole far above her, but their blinding glow no longer reached down into these cool dank depths. The path itself now wound down around and around this circular hole of hard smooth rock.

The click-click-click of her fox mount's claws against the slowly descending pathway, a ledge protruding from the wall and winding around and around, wider and wider.

Only the glow of her wonderful green spore lit the way now. Through what used to be the fox's eyes.

A glow that beamed brighter and brighter now that her demon core was reaching perfection.

This demon core, it was the last gift of her beloved mate before death finally claimed him forever. No hope of reviving him now. Not after that awful technique that boy used on him. That same technique that freed those clawgirls from her spore, from her control.

But power surged within her now. It was what she needed to not just claim the lives of that wrecked boy and his delusionally treacherous clawgirls, but all clawgirl kind.

A deep gust powered up through the circular hole.

A gust smelling of sweet brimstone and sweeter smoke.

That of her true masters: the baelzog.

Thanks to that wolf man, thanks to that undead wolf man using his own magical blade, all but the last locks on the baelzog had been severed.

Freed lesser baelzog from their prison. Lesser baelzog were already hunting down to punish those traitor clawgirls, and capture the boy that dared defy them and their minions.

Now for the last of the barriers.

Down deep below.

She cackled in glee at how her fox mount gnashed its fangs once again in well-deserved agony for daring move her less than her preferred trot. Her tentacles were now embedded within its skull, its brain, and her spore entrenched throughout its body.

And with that boy's curved blade held by her own tentacles nothing could free any more of her spored minions from her control.

Nothing.

And soon, this blade would free her true masters.

Be destroyed in the process.

And then her revenge would come—with nothing to interfere this time.

CHAPTER 6
ROMEO

Without another thought, Romeo bared his scimitar defensively in front of him. All the while gasping at the blinding gust of heat and smoke.

Dark red smoke.

Scolding both his skin and his breath. Already burning both the leaves and the wood torn away. The thick winding branch burned too. The bark. The smell. Like autumn, except fouled by some wrecked filthy bird beast.

A four-legged bird beast. Of dark smoke and dark red flame. Its body much like a cougar. But with wings of ash from its back. A head much like a giant hawk. With burning coals for amber fierce eyes.

It cackled birdishly.

Spat out another cock-a-doodle-do.

That must be Grif.

"No traitor left behind," Grif said, "That's what the Greater Baelzog wish."

The thing Romeo had thought was a man … no. Far from it.

It was two-legged, and roughly man-shaped, like a distorted brute of a man, with a twisted square of a brutal face, and yet all crimson smoke and even darker flame.

With a single giant eye. An eye of black-flamed coal.

That must be Midus.

"Ooo," Midus said, "Clawgirl ahoy! Yum yum. A fine-quality traitor to munch."

Midus even licked his chops with the darkest red tongue of flame Romeo could have imagined. A tongue as wide and thick as that wide crooked mouth.

And its fiery amber fangs.

CLANK!

Gif snapped his hooked hawkish beak over Romeo's scimitar.

Yanked it away. Right out of his hands.

"T-t-take," Velvet said, shuttering, whispering, "mine."

With a dash and grab, Romeo yanked out Velvet's other scimitar, and stood behind her, ready to defend her to the death.

But the bird beast of smoke and flame, Grif, chuckled again, along with that one-eyed man of flame and smoke, Midus.

Midus reached for the blade, but stopped so close by— strange, but Romeo didn't take the bait—yet.

"Ha!" Midus said, "As if our own weapons could ever harm us. See. Try it and despair, yum-yum boy."

Midus licked his chops again. Waiting.

Without anymore hesitation Romeo struck.

The blade swiped through the smoke and flame.

No contact. Nothing.

Useless—so far.

Midus and Grif laughed out loud, yet it was Midus that said, "Try again. Despair again!"

Listening to his own heart beat, the music of battle, Romeo steadied himself, and released a Slash-o-Boom.

Which passed right through both monsters.

Blasted a crater into the ground several paces behind them. The smell of vaporized ferns and rock stabbing the earthy smell of the forest.

No. No use here.

Romeo clenched his teeth. These monsters weren't undead, so forget his Puributcher technique.

One last technique that might work: Counter Kill Reversal Technique.

Yet Midus chuckled again.

"Still no despair?" he said, "One last try! Make it count!"

But that counter technique technique required physical contact, somehow, contact from a physical or magical attack …

So Puributcher it is—to make Midus attack, and then Counter Kill Reversal, to finish the job.

His skill, his practice of Puributcher coming true.

Let him flung the invisible purifying slashes quickly. Instinctively.

"Puributcher!" Romeo cried out, and flung the invisible flying slash technique through the monster's hand, and the wing of the bird beast Grif.

Making both parts explode. Flames gone. Smoke vanishing?

Both monsters howled.

And snarled for revenge.

CHAPTER 7
VIVIAN

Fighting through the pain lingering throughout her curled body from all those cock-a-doodle-dos, Vivian grabbed the dark red handle of the Savage Sword of Shadow Forest. This time its grip was solid, smooth, and yet soft. So much like the ivory feel of her now-lost pair of pink scimitars. Beautifully pink scimitars that got fused into this magical blade.

The bark underneath her thick bed of moss poked and jabbed her even more all of a sudden. Like nippy ants were trying to crawl up through her leotard and torment her.

Again and again.

The smell of brimstone, the biting smoke and flickering heat from below, a few paces to the side, where those two monsters of smoke and flame ... a four-legged cougar beast with a hawk's head and eagle wings, all dark black smoke and dark red and darker amber flames ... Vivian forced herself not to moan.

The smell of vaporized ferns. Of vaporized ground. Of charred stone.

Romeo was fighting them. No doubt about the chit-chat going on below.

Time to prove she wasn't so helpless.

Especially now—as the wielder of the Savage Sword of Shadow Forest.

Vivian yanked the blade out. The blade itself was too much like an evil deer antler, dark red, and curved wickedly.

A manly but scornful voice erupted in her head.

Challenging your former masters so soon?

What a dumb question. Of course she was! Vivian didn't even bother answered back.

Despite the rooster calls having kicked her in the gut, kicked her whole body everywhere weak and trembling, she forced herself to her feet.

Trembling already? Pathetic!

But Vivian knew better than to speak yet—and announce her presence to those monsters below.

A cyclops of flame and smoke. And a ... ah, a griffin. A cougar body. A hawk's head. And eagle wings. All in smoke and flame.

Except the cyclops was missing a forearm. The griffin was missing a wing.

Both snarled for vengeance.

Against Romeo?

Good.

Neither noticed Vivian—yet.

So she leapt.

Flying through the air.

Blade swinging down.

Through the cyclop's head. Massive glob of an eye.

Its scream cur off midway. its smoke puffing away. its flame flickering out forever.

All swallowed by her new sword? A sword that burned hot.

Too hot.

But Vivian refused to even whimper. Never let go.

Never.

Even as she landed hard on the branch beside Romeo and Velvet. The pain of her hard landing reverberated throughout her whole entire body. Each and totallies every bone.

Enough that she had to let out a gasp.

"Vivian!" Romeo called out.

And despite his ... dilly-dallying with Velvet these last few days, while completely totallies ignoring Vivian, Vivian, sigh, couldn't help but smile back at that lout.

"I'll protect you, Romeo," Vivian said, "Then—ack!"

The griffin snapped at her. Its biting brimstone breath blinding her for a moment.

A critical moment.

One that almost cost her hands and sword.

But her experience kicked in. And she leapt back just in time. Just far enough to dodge it.

Without falling off the thick winding branch.

"Curse you traitor!" the griffin said, "Your kind shall—AAAAAHHHHH!"

Its other wing exploded. Flames vanquished from its back.

Romeo snarled this time. "No touching my clawgirl girlfriends!"

That gave Vivian a smiled. Enough encouragement to leap again.

But midway realized her mistake.

The griffin pecked at her.

BANG!

Her sword shielded her. Barely.

But nothing deflected the Puributcher Technique that destroyed the griffin's head.

And her outfit, **again**.

CHAPTER 8

ROMEO

Romeo gasped at his bone-headed mistake, making his suede boots grip the bumpy bark of the winding thick branch even tighter.

Even with the bite of the brimstone smoke warming morning air even hotter, the smoldering ruins of the smaller branches and leaves where the bird-like beast Grif had swiped away the leaves and branches with its massive taloned claws, even now the cackling of fire below ... not good.

A forest fire, here, and now, a disaster of epic proportions. No hope of escape either.

But the ground was soggy with wetness. Leaves dank. Rock dark with moisture. Even that crater he made before with his Slash-o-Boom Technique showed plenty of muckiness of the wet kind.

Sure, Romeo looked away just in time. He didn't see

Vivian stark naked once again, but did that matter? He stripped her of her dignity and clothing *again*.

And her pouting heart of a face, no, he only needed to heat her cutesy annoyed grumble to know a smacking was coming his way.

Big time.

A well-deserved smacking.

And yet … crackle-crackle-crackle approaching him. Vivian. Bare foot and utterly naked—except for that savage looking blade of hers … even her lovely rosy fragrance, a natural musk that only grew stronger and stronger nowadays, Romeo couldn't help but tense.

Ready for the smacking of a lifetime.

Except … a warm sweet peck on his cheek.

"Vivian?" Romeo rasped(?) "I …"

"Silly boy," Vivian said, "I should have slept with you when we had the chance. Now with this silly no-sex-till-safe policy in place … I might as well embrace Velvet's approach to life—he-he."

Romeo … gulped. That cool tingle of her kiss … now warmer than any sun above this murky forest.

CHAPTER 9
MACKER THE CRUEL

Macker the Cruel held the legendary blade known as the Harp of Deathly Song. Its blade was like a crescent moon, but as black as the soul of the murderous sword itself. The sharp edge was on the inside of the curve, like a scythe of savage slaughter, but the metal itself was sleek and unscarred, despite eons of inflicting death and despair.

Even now, with his massive scaly hands, the blade was too small for him to wield, for any dragotroll to wield, and yet compelling that necromancer hobgobble, twisting her little squid mind to think she held this blade for herself in her hand tentacles, as if the blade would permit such an unworthy wielder to touch its handle and live.

Not that she would die—yet. She still had use. Right now she carried a different magical talisman.

One their true masters needed far more than this legendary blade.

And once this legendary blade rejected its last owner for infidelity, for daring to use blades other than this legendary blade, use too many inferior ones, than the boy was as good as dead.

No longer needed. A better wielder would be found. Bound to serve the true masters of this world.

But no need for that necromancer to know the truth, and endanger them all. The clawgirl who was chosen in this eon had betrayed them, but no need for her willing cooperation—if they could harvest her talons in the right way.

A truly painful and agonizing way.

But no. No need to risk that necromancer hobgobble's own treachery. Especially after so many clawgirls betrayed their cause.

Especially their own Chosen One.

The strong smell of spider and spider web carried thick in the rustling breeze, smothering out that awful fern and earthy muck. The smell of beautifully tasty and soft spider girl, of archnofey, of their treachery as well, soon to be punished with worse than mere death, but compelled service as the tormented undead.

The city of the archnofey was near.

More than enough demihumans had survived that bramble maze of death, and even his own axe ambush at the end. Those who did survive had been revived as undead minions of that necromancer hobgobble—least for now, as hard-to-kill fodder.

Fodder wouldn't die so easily. More like wouldn't stay dead so easily.

Those who survived were lined up in rows before him. Plenty of beautifully tasty-looking bunny girls—looking all too human except for their bunny tails and ears, but also foxling with their fox ears and tails, even bearlings and tiger-ling, and more than a few wolfings.

All armed with the best of their preferred weapon.

With the best brigandine.

They were sergeants now, who'd lead their undead lessers into battle soon.

Very soon.

Along with those land squids known as hobgobbles. They and their own lords would be honored with the first wave of attack, and the wave most likely, in the end, to break through, if the plan worked out closely enough to reality.

But no plan survived reality completely intact ...

Macker the Cruel would soon provide plenty of delicious archnofey flesh for their true masters to feast on. Regain their strength and former powers.

And begin the true invasion.

Begin the end of mankind—as anything but livestock.

CHAPTER 10

ROMEO

R omeo gulped.

It wasn't just the morning air now heating up like crazy. His whole entire body ... good thing his jerkin was red, because his whole entire body must be blushing redder than ... than ... gulp.

The winding thick branch couldn't give them much comfortable ... fun time, but if ... well ... the cool tingle on his cheek was any sign ... a bare utterly nude Vivian ... an hourglass beauty to his own deserved doom—if he violated that no-sex-till-safe policy, especially in front of Velvet here, but ... Vivian so eager rather than so angry ...

The wind rustled the ferns below. Blowing away the last of that brimstone stink. Away with the last of the recent danger.

Danger both Romeo and Vivian felled together.

Like true allies and even truer lovers and ... you know.

So, of course, standing so cutesy before him like a steaming hot peach pie for the eyes and loins, Vivian stared at him longingly with her big bright violet eyes, and how her long lush rosy pink hair framed her lovely oval face and yet also pouted cutesy at him and yet her hair also covered her buxom big chest, so, okay, not entirely naked, right?

But no missing how much stronger her natural rosy fragrance was compared to a few days ago back when they were sleeping with each other in the same tree, but fully dressed.

And still more beautiful than any rose.

Especially with the breeze adding an extra tingle of rose toward him.

Velvet, with a knowing giggle, slipped her hand to his sword one ... and took back her scimitar?

With another knowing giggle?

"Enjoy ..." Velvet said. "And I'll go ... you know ..."

And with a swoosh, carrying a gust of almond and vanilla musk to his back, Velvet vanished, no doubt fetching her other scimitar and scouting for any other dangers nearby while ... you know.

Romeo wasn't the only one to gulp this time.

Yet Vivian also pouted?

"This stupid blade," she said, "totallies thinks you're more worthy than me, just because you're a guy."

Romeo huffed. "Stupid blade is wrong. You—"

Vivian grabbed his other hand. Pressed it against her breast? and wow, it was so soft, warm, and and and ... gulp.

"Undress," Vivian said, her cutesy pout deepening, "It's

only fair. You saw me naked likey totallies **twice**, and I haven't ... totallies you know. No fair."

"You're right," he said, and his other hand unbuttoned his jerkin.

Stroked her face.

"Would you," he said, "show me your clawgirl form too?"

Vivian looked downcast. "I ..."

She gulped, loud and nervous.

But he kissed her full on the strawberry sweet lips.

"No worries," he said, "if you're not ready for that ..."

He gulped, cupping her oval face, her cheek so gently, like her many kittens she used to care for, before Aunt Tilda put her foot down and got rid of them all.

"You sure," he said, "if we, you know, in your current form that ..."

He gulped again, but she kissed him back. Full on the lips. With a cutesy moan. Warming him hotter than any beam of sunlight ever could.

"That," she said, "I think. Just dime dreadful nonsense. Right? They also totallies said all clawgirls likey me, well, all seduce and slay, and no, well, likey ... heart."

She kissed him back. Staying even closer this time. Her breath as warm and rosy fragrant as the rest of her now.

"You have plenty of heart, tons of it," he said, and slipped his free hand across the nap of her back, but she grimaced.

Her giggle. "Your pants?"

"You want to?" he said, "Or ..."

Vivian giggled, happy, but still too nervous.

"I can likey unbutton buttons," she said, and giggled even

more sinister, "quicker than you ever totallies imagined, but will your buttons even survive?"

"On second thought ..." Romeo said, "My clothes won't regenerated from damage like—ack!"

A snap. His pants were reaaaaaally too loose now, and fell to his ankles.

"Oopsie!" Vivian said, and giggled even more.

Sigh.

"I should have known ..." Romeo said, but before he could finish, Vivian pressed herself against him.

So soft.

So heart-thunkingly warm.

With a sultry pant and moan, she fit on him like the perfect sheath embracing his manhood blade. A blade that he kept thrusting into her, and she kept moaning yes yes yes yes ... more more more ....

Until his seed speared into her and she gasped in utter excited relief.

Holding him tight, Vivian sighed again.

Whispered into his ear.

"I still love you," she said, "as much as before, no, even more now—he-he. Totallies more. Now this time ... let's totallies make our future wormlings feel our love."

Kids with Vivian ... somehow, his heart clenched and yet ... deep down.

"Lots of wormlings," he said.

CHAPTER II
JULIET

J uliet grumbled at those distant pants and moans of disgusting pleasure that completely and utterly meant Vivian was fucking Romeo, **finally**, but after everyone's no-sex-till-safe agreement a few days ago?

Really?

Now?

Juliet was only a few trees over. Several dozen paces away *at* **most**. Well, accounting for all the winding thick branches, all the wide pointy leaves bunched together that only kinda hid them all and rustling way too loudly and scrappy in the breeze. A breeze that was still getting hotter and hotter, despite all the dank murk still around her.

That so many songbirds kept chirping their little birdie brains out even as Romeo and Vivian clearly and loudly were consummating their annoyingly sudden newfound love, too much like back when Romeo first fucked Juliet rather than claim her for a bounty that ... Romeo could have claimed them all for high bounties but choose girlfriending them so sigh.

And having packmates again ... packmates that actually cared for her ... it was nice, actually.

Even if she was stuck wearing this stupid lightning-blue leotard with pink lightning bolts patterned over it far too suggestively.

And stupider thigh boots in the same style, just like her bracers and ugh, icky icky human-bone scimitars of lightning blue with, well, nice pink handles that, why she knew how to use them when she never used a sword before, how to fire their magical bolts halfway decently ... ugh.

But no doubt Vivian hadn't shown Romeo her clawgirl form, yet.

Romeo had just loved Juliet's clawgirl form. They fucked so many times ... and he still wanted her in his human form too, sort of, probably, still, it's just that, now, with so many packmates eager to have him too ... sigh.

No.

Focus.

She had to protect them. Help protect them. While her dragon daddy was off bringing Fleur and Claudia to that Archnofey Village somewhere in Shadow Forest nearby to get help, to see if they'd be granted safe harbor, at least for a little while.

Yet—huh?!

That stink of rotting fish ... from up here. In the canopy? Not the ground. The canopy!

Juliet whipped out her scimitars. Heart racing stupid fast. Battle music, Romeo had called it, but this was nothing like a dance. No one tried to kill you when you danced.

Flashes of disgusting dark blue and dark brown? A few dozen paces away. Scattered within the bunch of leaves.

Juliet snapped the pommels of her scimitars together.

Screamed: "Hobgobbles incoming!"

Just as she loosed several magical arrows cackling with blue lightning their way.

Missing all of them? No!

Dark blur flung toward her.

Spears!

She had to dodge. Quickly!

But she stumbled. Backwards.

And—

CRACK!

Velvet landed on the closest. Pouncing it like a leopard. Hopping in front of Juliet.

Her scimitar bow loosing violet bolts.

Exploding the other spears.

Velvet giggled as smoothly as her namesake.

"Leave this trash to me," Velvet said, "Go watch over our Romeo and Vivian."

Juliet stammered. "B-b-but!"

"Vivian only has that strange sword," Velvet said, and loosed several more bolts. Destroyed several more spears. "and Romeo is completely unarmed."

"Oh," Juliet said, and gulped, lowing her own scimitar bow, "Yeah. I'll go. Now."

"Hurry," Velvet said, "There's more trouble on the way, and quickly."

More than quickly ... what the wind carried ... it wasn't just hobgobble that was stinking up the air now.

CHAPTER 12
ROMEO

Romeo pressed his bare back against Vivian's just as Juliet screamed out "Hobgobbles incoming!"

His slacks hung a few paces away, off this very same thick winding branch, but at least his sueded boots still griped the bark of the limb tightly, unlike Vivian, who was bare footed as well.

The smaller branches and leaves only provided so much cover now, and none in the direction those strange smoke and flame creatures had attacked them from.

But no doubt what that rotting fish stink meant.

But the cries that sounded half-human, half-beast? Wait. Demihumans. Like humans but with bestial parts, like beast ears, tail, and sometimes claws.

If only Romeo had a blade. Even a broken branch. Something.

Better than being bare handed.

Completely dependent on Vivian.

Who giggled super happy.

"This time," Vivian said, "I totallies get to protect you—he-he."

"And do it," Romeo said, "mutually butt naked."

"I am so," Vivian said, "developing a technique as perverted and totallies nasty as your Puributcher soon—"

Flickers of dark brown leather a dozen paces away. In the trees. Not the ground.

Dark blue flickers. Flashes of dark blue flesh similar to the rotting blueberries ma once had him plant all over the—ack!

The big round heads of hobgobbles popped out the clusters of leaves a dozen paces away. With gaping toothy maws splitting the head horizontally like wicked scimitars. No eyes, yet their eyesight was somehow amazing, least according to the dime dreadfuls, and his limited experience agreed so far. A few tentacles up for arms. Other thicker tentacles instead of legs.

But these hobgobbles wore what looked like armor. Dark brown leather. Strapped over some of their head and body. Exactly like armor.

Multiple upper tentacles each held a wicked dark metal spear, each ready to be flung at incredible speeds and power.

Romeo readied his fists. What little good that would do, it was better than nothing.

"No more sword-swarm maging?" he said.

"Not yet," Vivian said, "but I'll figure it out against soon enough."

"Soon?" he said, "Before these hobgobbles strike?"

"I wish," Vivian said.

"Me too," he said, "Cut a branch for me."

Vivian sighed, and a wooden wallop erupted behind him. Then a few more.

"Anything totallies is better than nothing," she said, and slipped him a wooden ... blade? No. A sword. No hilt. Just a one-sided blade and handle. Razor amber sharp blade, a pace long and deadly. And a foot or so of dark gray solid bark. Its weight, solid, and balanced decently.

All smelling of freshly sliced wood.

"Nice wood working," Romeo said, and readied the sword.

Vivian giggled again. "I learned from the best."

"Who was that?" Romeo said.

"Guess."

"Wood Goddess of Shadow Forest. No doubt about it."

"No silly. Boss Tilda."

"*Really?*"

"Yeah."

More flashes close and closer of filthy-blueberry blue and dark brown leather and even a glimpses of dark metal.

Enough to chill the heat of the morning away nicely.

"I never knew ..." Romeo said.

"Lots you didn't, silly," Vivian said.

Less than a dozen paces away now. Hobgobbles hidden obviously among the clusters of leaves. None in the open.

Yet.

None attack--yet.

A glance downward and ....
Oh crap.

43

CHAPTER 13

ROMEO

Romeo now had a hunch why the hobgobbles were gathering less than a dozen paces around him and Vivian, surrounding them throughout the thick winding branches, but no open attacks.

Yet.

Because down below, hidden partially among the ferns and among the big craggy boulders were humans with bestial ears and tails. From wolves, to bears, and even foxes and squirrels and um, bunny men, but ... no bunny girls?

All in bloodied leather tunics. Ripped in different places. Some worse than others. Underneath the tunics their gambeson were ripped too. Damaged almost as badly.

Yet their flesh looked unscarred.

Unwounded?

No blood was splattered along the ferns either. Or

scrapped onto them. Just snaps. Of the ferns' stems and leaves breaking.

A chill tingled down Romeo's spine. Least Vivian's back to his own helped keep that chill under control.

Since there were no caws of crows nearby. No sign of any bird. Not even songbirds.

But in the distance ... plenty of caws.

Yet here. Close by ...

Just hobgobbles gathering around them. Like a school of tree squids about to swarm them like Romeo and Vivian were a pair of delicious little tree minnows.

Demihumans gathering below them. Ready to harass them from below. Ensure they couldn't escape from the hobgobbles' coming assault.

But their main scheme haunted the tip of Romeo's tongue.

"Vivian, any ideas—"

"Don't attack yet. It's a trap. Getting out ... follow my lead."

"Ready when you are."

CHAPTER 14
JULIET

Juliet dashed down the wide winding branch, trying her best not to slip on the thick dank moss and not stumble over the countless bumps of bark. All while keeping the thunks of her thigh boots as quiet as she could and surprise, surprise, she actually could stay kinda quiet without trying too hard.

Clawgirl instincts were actually helpful. Sometimes.

Ahead the flashes of icky disgusting choked-blue hiding among the pointy broad leaves ... hobgobbles!

That rotting fish stink ... she didn't dare cry out. Forget trying to command them like she used to be able to. For some reason that never worked at all anymore. Ever since that necromancer hobgobble used her spore on Juliet, it did something to her that Romeo's technique wasn't able to undo.

But those hobgobbles surrounded Romeo and Vivian. A

deep breath, and a hint of yummy boy flesh that she'd never ever even nibble on.

Yeah. Romeo was there.

But a wall of blue tree squid blocked the way. Bristling with dark metal spears far sharper than her own talons in her clawgirl form, and she was in her human form right now.

At least none were facing her—yet.

They hadn't noticed her—yet.

Despite her quiet panting she raced closer and closer. Her heart raced at the thought of fighting so many hobgobbles.

But Romeo and Vivian had it worse.

Romeo was unarmed, and Vivian only had that strange ugly sword.

Least Juliet had both scimitars. Both snapped together and ready to fire her lightning bolts with, but ...wait.

Down below ... people with beast ears and tails?

No ... demihumans!

If only Juliet had spoken more to Azura, that weird panicky bunny girl before ... wait.

Where was Azura?!

BOOOOMMMMM!!!!!

The whole tree shook. Nearly shaking her off like a dog shaking off a flea.

And not just this tree. The whole forest?!

Plenty of hobgobbles even fell to the ground. Splattering, but then recovering?

Getting up!

Undead hobgobbles!

"Stay away from my Romeo!!!!"

Azura! Yes!

They all stood a chance after all.

Azura carried a giant heavy hammer and must have started the fight to save Romeo and Vivian without anyone asking her to.

(Phew.)

Maybe Romeo did have a good sense of monster girls like Juliet and the others.

Juliet hopped down. Landed on the dark soggy soil. Trying her best not to snap any of the fragile ferns. Scrap them too loudly.

She headed toward Azura. Her voice. The booms. Hopping between boulders now like a grasshopper desperate to avoid the notice of a huddled pack of praying mantises …

Cries of beasts and—a girl's scream?

Azura!

"No! No! No!" Azura screamed. "How can you still be alive! How can you … you come back to life?! Noooooo! Not fair!"

Ugh.

Juliet growled at the stupid bunny girl. They had told her about that hobgobble necromancer but … sigh, Azura had already even known too. Supposedly. Least according to what she said.

Several wolf men popped out ahead of Juliet. Big men with wolf ears and tails. And big sharp but straight swords.

Until she shot both in the chest. Through the heart. With her lightning arrows.

Fried them both good.

Stinking of long awful dead wolf roasted too.

They both collapsed. No doubt they'd recover. Undead anything was just the worse, but Juliet charged passed them. Hopping bounder over boulder.

When more wolf men lunged out at her.

More lightning arrows from her.

More wolf men fried paralyzed and stinky.

BOOOOOOMMMMM!!!!!

Close by. Shaking the ground. Enough to make Juliet stumble. Nearly fall. But she caught herself on a stubby low stone. Like a stepping stone.

A lucky stone.

BOOM!

BOOM!

BOOM!

Juliet called out. "Azura?!"

But it wasn't Azura who answered her.

CHAPTER 15

ROMEO

Romeo waited for several moments, waiting with only his suede boots on gripping the thick branch, bare butt naked with his back against Vivian and her bare utterly naked back.

Yet Vivian hadn't moved—yet.

Taking a deep breath ... her rosy fragrance was stronger now, but not unpleasant. It was the hobgobble rotting fish stink that was unpleasant. Full of unpleasant memories.

Especially for Vivian, from the tension in her back.

BOOM!

BOOM!

BOOM!

From below. A good dozen paces away.

Romeo called out: "Azura?"

"No," Vivian said, "I don't think it's her. She's—"

"WAAAAAAAAHHHHH! I don't want to diiiiiiieeeee!"

Vivian sighed. "Okay, *that's* Azura."

The whiny but busty beautiful bunny girl was hidden, so far, by countless leaves and smaller branches to his side.

Howl and yowls erupted behind them. Along with the wet cracking of bone against solid heavy hammer.

"Sooooorrrriiiiieeeee," Azura said, "but—"

The other demihumans screamed, "TRAITOR!"

Least more wet cracking sounds—she smacked even more of those demihumans away.

"Don't worry," she said, "my hammer can't kill you guys, so just—"

"DEATH CANNOT STOP US!"

A bunch of them were right below Romeo. A little to his side.

Time for Puributcher—wooden blade edition.

They all screamed. Shocked. In agony.

Then thumps.

Silence.

"Romeo!" Vivian said, "Now those hobgobbles will—"

"I'll dis-armor them," Romeo said, "and you finished them off."

More Puributcher. More ... wait.

The hobgobbles hit by the technique shrieked.

Fell unmoving?

"They're all undead!" Romeo said.

And with some more Puributchers not a single evil undead minion was left alive.

Nor, from the glimpses between the countless leaves, was a certain whiny but busty gorgeous bunny girl still at all clothed ...

CHAPTER 16

KROTHA RIGOT

K rotha finally reached the bottom of this endless abysmal hole. A hole so dank and dark, so homely and yet the smell of brimstone, of her true masters lingering here close by, but for far too long ...

Not even the gleam of those glowing spider webs reached down here to these deep dark depths. No. Just cool soothing darkness above. The ledge she had circled around was now gone. Vanished as if it never had been.

Least for her.

For now.

The floor was flat. Smoother than a razor fine spear, and just as narrow and straight. The fox Krotha rode on glowed just enough through the spore in its eyes to light the way. But the pathway was almost as black as the endless abyss surrounding the narrow pathway. The utmost care had to be taken or else ... no.

Failure was unimaginable.

And that's when the doorway appeared before her.

A doorway unlike anything she had ever experienced.

So vast it was beyond her comprehension. Darker black than the abyss surrounding the narrow pathway. As dark as a demon core—like the very demon core within her!

Yet the power ... trembling, she was trembling with ... with excitement. Pure hope. Her clan ... it will be avenged.

And all of humanity will despair.

CHAPTER 17
JULIET

Out of a patch of craggy boulders nearly a dozen paces ahead of Juliet, some beautifully tall, ruby-haired bunny girl in slutty green brigandine hopped out instead of Azura.

Standing tall on the highest of the jagged boulders the ruby-haired bunny girl was ready to wield a massive skeletal-themed hammer held with both her slim hands. Those fiercely jealous green eyes of hers, too much like the shredded bits of ferns scattered around the boulders.

The ruby-haired bunny girl's pout matched her fierce glare. Fierce enough to burn through the murk and—ack!

More howls behind Juliet!

Several dozen paces away. At the closest.

She really needed to hurry … but this annoyingly tall bunny girl blocked the way to Romeo and Vivian. Their voices, their chit chat, they were so close too. Up in the thick craggy oak tree ahead.

But the awful bunny girl announced herself and her intentions right away.

"Killing so many of my undead wolves," she said, "You'll pay for that. Just like you'll pay for betraying us, clawbrat."

Juliet didn't dignify that nonsense with words.

Just several lightning bolts at that busty bitch's chest.

But the bunny bitch dodged them easily? As if Juliet's aim was off.

Way off.

But her aim was never *that* off.

The ruby-haired bunny bitch smashed a boulder. Like that annoying game known as golf that patrons had loved far, far, faaaaar too much.

The bunny girl smashed the boulder into extra huge shards. Then swung her manner, smacking the shards, flinging them all at Juliet.

And so quick Juliet had to lunge away.

Roll away.

But no, she wasn't fast enough.

Several shards smashed right into Juliet. She yelped. In pain. Her side. Her back. Skin scales marred badly—and she just molted only days ago!

But she was alive, for now. Thanks to her leotard's real actual protection, somehow.

The stink of chalk. From the broken boulders?

The bunny bitch cackled. "Who said you get to die quickly? That's too good for you, clawbrat."

SMASH!

Another boulder destroyed. More rocky shrapnel. Too fast. Juliet couldn't dodge all of it.

Those cracks. Not just rock against her. But wet ones. Inside her.

Her yelps. Tears. Pain. Real. Agonizing. *pain.*

More scornful laughs from that bunny bitch.

And nothing Juliet could do—unless ... gulp.

Clawgirl time?

Crouching, legs wobbling, Juliet snapped her scimitar bow apart and sheathed the scimitars.

Just as another smash-crack rang out.

The bunny bitch's next attack.

No. Juliet shifted. No other choice.

No matter the paint. The severe pain. The gasps for breath.

Her peachy skin seemed to stretch, but in fact, changed to lovely pink scales. Exotic scales. High bounty to the wrong kind of people. Her hands and feet into eagle-style talons with ruby red claws. Her teeth into fangs.

Razor sharp fangs.

And all hungry for that bunny girl now.

Pink lightning cackled between her hand claws. With ruby flames flickering with the bolts of lightning.

"Time for some fried bunny girl," Juliet said.

But the bunny bitch smirked. "Good-bye, clawbitch."

And she slung the hammer over her slim shoulder?

"Giving up," Juliet said, "Ha! I won't—ah!"

Wolf howls right behind her?

Oh no!

"Rip her apart," the bunny bitch said, and then licked her chops, "but save the heart for me and me alone."

The wolf men all howled a yeeeeees!

Juliet spun around.

Struck them with her lightning. Frying the first few.

No.

Several.

But even more took their places.

More fried to the ground.

More taking their places.

Including those she fried a round ago.

Juliet backed up more and more but ...

"This is it for you," the bunny bitch said, "Chosen Trait—ACK! No ... impossible ... my luck."

A thump. The bunny girl dead?

Dropping the wolves too?

And a velvety voice chuckled above them.

"Has run out."

CHAPTER 18
ROMEO

Romeo rubbed his cheek again. It flared with pain and heat. More heat than any hot sun could ever beam on it. His teeth even felt ... achy. Loose.

All because Azura, when suddenly naked, got very, very slappy with him. His cheek now was **very** familiar with her slim hand, and its incredible strength.

And not in a sexy way.

Not at all.

Never mind they had slept with each other already. Soon after meeting the first time even. So why ...

Sigh.

Back in his slacks but no red jerkin this time, Romeo leaned against what must have been the lumpiest bearded oak in the forest, but he still savored the soft thick moss against his bare back.

Eyes shut for now, of course, despite Azura and Vivian

being behind the tree, they both were now "fixing" his red jerkin to be the clothing Azura very much needed some of right now.

Their whispers were barely above the rustles of the ferns. Rustles from the hot breeze blowing through the murk. Few those whispers were ... kind. Overusing his perverted Puributcher technique was clearly the topic, and how to get him to stop, was probably the other topic, and argued even more fiercely.

The breeze was nearly still, and for awhile too and yet ... wait ... the ferns, they were shifting, swaying without a breeze, and that sweeping sway was coming closer and closer.

The smell of spider?

Lots and lots of spider. The cackling of damp leaves underneath the ferns too.

From countless little stabbing legs.

"Um ... Vivian, Azura ..." Romeo said.

"Hush, my lovely."

Right into his ear. Right beside him?

Lots of grumbles and harsh whispers from Azura and Vivian, and neither seemed eager to acknowledge his presence at the moment.

Best listen.

Romeo nodded. Silently.

Since that hint of lilies and lemonade scent confirmed it was someone familiar. Trust his nose and his nose said he was familiar with her, in a good way.

Probably.

Except for those glimpses of the approaching horde of spiders. Giant black widows. Each as big as his own hand. All with a red skullish thing on their backs.

Worse than the nightmares of being trapped in some dungeon style attic and—wait.

Wasn't their red thing different before?

Then again, a lot happened. He couldn't really remember the last time, if there was a last time even.

"Time to go to my village," the girl said, "and this time, no detours."

Romeo knew better than to ask who she was but ...

He whispered. "Detours?"

"Your memories," she said, "they haven't come back yet, have they?"

"No."

"Good. Let's go. Before your luggage notices."

Luggage?

But he nodded. No telling how Vivian and Azura would react right now if he said anything. And with them rearing to fight ... especially fight him ... no telling how this new girl would react either.

Or this horde of spiders.

"Let's go ..." he said.

"Veuve Noire, my little Romeo."

CHAPTER 19

MACKER THE CRUEL

The smoldering ashes of black and crimson slag piled before Macker the Cruel revealed the danger that the boy and his treacherous girls had proven to be.

The pile was like a deformed log pile up stacked to his knees, and yet it was a combination of two precious but lesser baelzog. The least of the lot, but still among the true masters.

Just the smell, of ash and death, of flame and destruction, it was potent but not potent enough to paralyze the truly strong.

Macker gnashed his fangs.

The invasion must be halted for a funeral. Even for a day. Merely a day, but a memorial to remind these fodder the real reason why they exist to serve, serve and die as many times and their masters wished them to revive, that and only that.

The traitors must be brought to their knees, forced to obey, serve, and then die many times in endless agony for daring to do anything else.

An eternity of agony as an example to others.

Time for the preparations.

The timing was good, as awful as the situation was. His spies within the archnofey village needed more time to be effective. Soon that last village of traitors would fall.

The last of many hills to overcome—until the invasion, no, *massacre* of the human world could commence.

"Macker?"

A girl's voice, but full of sultry flame and determination. The smell of ash and flame, with strangely sweet hints of cherry and vanilla and even autumn.

Time to be a good example to the fodder he led.

He bowed toward her voice. Not even he was worthy of looking at her stunning grace and deadly beauty.

Not without explicit permission.

"Yes, my Mistress."

She giggled so pleasantly.

"Oh, my beloved sweet Macker," she said, "are the rest of the fodder ready?"

"As ready as you wish them to be," he said, bowing even deeper, pleased to help her laugh so delighted.

Let the other fodder understand the truth of their existence.

"Good," his Mistress said, "Ravage the archnofey village to the ground. Enjoy the traitors and their flesh in the way you most desire, but spare the loyal. Grant them easy deaths and revive them to serve in death—as punishment for failing to stop the treachery of their kindred."

"As you wish, my Mistress."

"And these clawgirls that betrayed us," his Mistress said, and then sighed, " to think I fashioned such creatures myself, and yet they'd reject that honor by ... by ... those wretches, sigh. I'll deal with them myself and ..."

The sound of steps coming closer and closer to him?

"Macker, you looked concerned ..."

"Mistress," he said, "Two of the Beloved Baelzog were slain by that lot. To go yourself, without—"

But his Mistress cackled so loud and pleasantly shocked he couldn't continue.

"I've heard, I've heard," his Mistress said, "That a mere *human* boy slew my ex's, but a boy with such perverted tasted in women ..."

His Mistress took a deep sultry breath, but Macker dared only bow deeper and deeper. So deep he was breathing in the dark soil.

"Time to show him the truth nature of our kind," his Mistress said, "Let him savor my beauty and despair. That and the archnofey village ..."

Suddenly his Mistress cackled so loud and happy, Macker feared too much for her safety yet knew better than to speak.

Yet.

"Ah," his Mistress said, "a nice little plan I have too, and that boy could be key."

And the plan, his role in it, Macker was partly relieved.

But only partly.

The risk to his Mistress ... too great to ignore, but it was not his place to question her. Only aid her in any way she saw fit.

"As you wish, my Mistress."

CHAPTER 20

ROMEO

Romeo counted the bearded oaks—one hundred and one, one hundred and two, one hundred and ... and ... sigh.

Again.

The ferns were far too many to bother counting. No trail, not even a deer trail, showed the way right now, and the dark murk was only getting darker, thicker, like a heavy curtain without a single sunbeam poking through.

Only the biggest black widow Romeo had the mispleasure of following—a spider three times as big as Romeo himself—but he knew better than to do anything but smile gently and hope that he'd eventually get to see this Vueve Noir, who seemed to be following right behind him.

Hopefully she wasn't simply a big female spider either. Anyway, what spider would smell of lemonade anything? None, that's what, so don't worry.

Much.

Hopefully spiders couldn't scent fear, or else they'd know that, despite the muggy heat, even without his jerkin, he was chillier than Juliet used to be toward him at the Honey Heart Resort.

The rustle and snaps of ferns behind him sounded as if the figure of Vueve Noir wasn't so different as his own.

Yeah. Keep hope alive and well. No telling what he'd have to do if she wasn't human-looking enough. Clawgirls, despite their reptilian form, still looked plenty human, despite their eagle-style talons for hands and feet, and their scaled bodies, but wow, were their bodies amazingly feminine.

Gorgeously feminine.

And looks weren't skin deep.

Well, not scale deep in their case.

His heart pounded with each and every step further from Vivian and Azura he took. Even if he wanted to turn back, he'd have no idea where to go.

Least no monsters came at any of them. Yet. Apparently a big black widow was scary enough for the monsters here in this forest. Maybe. Hopefully.

But that sudden howl so far off.

Maybe not.

A hallow wolfish howl quiet from distance but it suddenly swerved to reptilian snarling screech of hungry rage and echoed everywhere, despite its far distance away.

The giant spider slowed down. Turned to the side.

And hurried off.

Romeo moved to follow—until a hand covered his

mouth. A strong hand, holding him in place, yet slim and soft and smelling strongly of lemonade.

"Hush, my little Romeo," Vueve Noir said, "The Gantzry comes and it's closer than it sounds."

Romeo nodded, but Vueve Noir continued, without releasing his mouth.

"Not even my greatest spider," she said, "can save us if it catches us here in the open."

Romeo tightened his grip on his own wooden blade. A blade Vivian carved for him so recently, but even his greatest techniques couldn't cut down the worst of foes if his blade wasn't strong enough to handle the pressure of the technique.

"No blade will save us," she said, "but the thought was so sweet of you."

A moist peck against the back of his neck, from lips juicy and humanly girlish sweet.

"For that," she said, "I have an idea. Gorloch will risk herself to draw the Gantzry off for a little bit more. While we go on a more dangerous route. A route that even the Gantzry fears to take—but where your blade might prove our salvation."

A challenge worthy of a guy with dwarf blood then.

So this time Romeo placed one hand over the one over his mouth, and gave hers a sweet little peck in return.

Her sweet giggle—sweeter than any lemonade ever.

CHAPTER 21
JULIET

Juliet did her best not to grumble at Romeo and his stupidly trusting nature, but sheesh, couldn't he at least **question** whether some pretty monster girl was, in fact, actually not so pretty on the inside.

Ever?

Really ...

As flattering as it was to be trusted at all by a guy, especially after revealing her true nature in such a ... sigh.

Maybe that was it. It worked out so well, so far but the moment it didn't ... would he ever trust any of them again?

The thick winding branches let Juliet and Velvet trail Romeo and that annoyingly pretty spider girl that Velvet called a archnofey.

They weren't just behind them. They were several dozen paces to the side too.

Yet the ferns hid that spider girl's bottom half all too well.

But the rustling and swaying the ferns suggested a regular pair of legs.

Not a spider bottom.

Her black swallowtail butterfly wings looked so lovely, even with those red bucktail patterns. Patterns that were just like her many black spiders trailing them.

Or even that huuuuuge black spider leading them to ... somewhere.

Somewhere that might not be any good.

No.

Not might. Probably.

Juliet already had her scimitars snapped together as a bow. Ready to feather and electrocute that spider fairy blonde.

Right in the gap of her neck.

Through her shoulder-length blonde wedges of hair. But that pair of red locks framed a slim pixie pretty face that no doubt Romeo would drool stupid and stupider over, especially over those big brilliant green eyes.

How she found such a nice red and black high neck minidress, how it sheened nice and clean in the dirty murk, despite the lack of sunbeams or even real light.

Ugh.

Even with the reptilian boost natural to her own eyesight, Juliet struggled to make out Romeo or the girl behind him in this murk.

But if that archnofey girl, as Velvet called her, had been at the resort, she'd well ... be Juliet's foremost rival in looks, even if not in height, in, gulp.

Just her voice was mesmerizing and Juliet never managed *that* with her own voice.

It even lured the birds and squirrels to ignore the many, many spiders and settle down too close and listen to those words until their awful sudden deaths.

Deaths Romeo never noticed because they all happened behind him.

Well behind him.

But not Juliet. Between her and that awful archnofey girl.

When suddenly a spooky howl of some huge-sounding wolf erupted in the distance.

A howl that turned ... turned ... that was no wolf!

It was so shrill and ... a dragon? Like her father?

Yet that cringe deep down ... definitely not her father. No.

The big spider veered off.

Dashed toward ... toward ... Juliet and Velvet!

But Velvet grabbed her arm. Shook her head.

Mouthed—*don't.*

Then hushed Juliet silent?

But Juliet nodded. Humored her for now.

Even when that blonde spider girl looked back at them, and smirked up, all sinister and sly, while holding their Romeo from behind as like he was a little fly to be wrapped up and drained dry very, very soon.

Yet she mouthed: *fight it—or else ...*

The blonde spider girl licked her chops, and fangs, and snuggled against Romeo even more.

The threat clear.

But she motioned not toward her overgrown spider, but toward the source of the howl?!

Juliet gaped, pouted, but ... sigh, nodded.

The blonde spider girl mouthed: *See you all soon—if you survive.*

And her smirk—as if the next time would be far, far worse.

CHAPTER 22

ROMEO

Despite forcing a small smirk, Romeo couldn't help but gulp at the sight before him.

A gaping wide maw of stone led deep into the earth. Into darkness as dank and disturbing as an ancient grave of some forgotten kingdom haunted by death and despair. Thick roots curled around the giant opening, and hung their jagged ends all along and passed the edge. The stone was all too much like curled lips and the roots, like sharp fangs frozen horribly in time.

Especially the many broken bones scattered around it. Woven throughout the roots. As if the roots were feeding on the marrow in the bones. If there still was marrow in those bleached bones.

But many of those bones were big and thick, as if from powerful beasts. Along with plenty of skulls from human-like creatures, even if some were clearly less than human. Maybe even more reptilian than a clawgirl in her scary form. Many were broken in some way.

No wonder the Gantzry hesitated to go inside that thing.

Only the solid unbroken lichen and moss all over the rock and roots confirmed the opening wasn't a genuine maw, or, at least, it hadn't moved since forever.

Another hallow wolfish howl. From far behind them. Ringing up into a reptilian screeching snarl that echoed everywhere ... closer and closer.

Except in the dark maw of an opening?

Stranger and stranger.

But Vueve Noir still had her slim beautiful hand over his mouth. Gentle but firmly there.

Another hand was on his shoulder. Guiding him gently but just as firmly.

But his back ... it savored the bliss of perky big breasts poking his shoulder blades oh-so-softly and rubbing them more gently than ... than ... brainfart.

The best kind of brainfart.

The fabric on those breasts as smoother, finer than silk and trapped the warmth there just fine. Aunt Tilda would kill to snag some of that kind of cloth for her girls at the resort. If Romeo could return with some of it, maybe, *maybe* Aunt Tilda would forgive him for vanishing for a few days.

Maybe.

But not likely. She would be so worried by now. That so many of her girls vanished too ... would she have sent a search party for them all?

Maybe.

Maybe not. No telling if she'd risk letting the patrons know there was something wrong, and as perverted and lustful as they were, they'd discover the truth sooner or later, so maybe asking the right patrons for recommendations ... while paying for the search itself ... sigh.

Aunt Tilda would definitely send a search party.

Maybe not the first day missing, but by now—yeah.

Definitely.

But the warm breath of Vueve Noir warming the back of his neck, sending his heart racing stupider and stupider, Aunt Tilda would no doubt shake her head, and smack him for being too lustful and stupid.

Even more lustful than the worst patrons.

The crash of ferns and the snap of branches behind them ... the sound of a big bulk was coming, and coming quickly?

Yet Vueve Noir didn't hurry any faster.

No.

She ...

"My dear Gorloch," Vueve Noir said, "So many legs lost. So many new scars. We must hurry. The Gantzry is not far behind. And Gorloch had refused to flee until we are safely within the Maw of Heated Echo."

Romeo nodded. Kept going. Letting Vueve guide him. His memory of her ... he knew her but from where? That trust he had in her was so strong and yet so ... his memory didn't match his trust and yet ... no.

Now's not the time to question her.

If she was false—as unlikely as that would be—his blade would save him.

Probably.

Another howl ripped through the murk.

A howl that veered into a reptilian screech all too soon.

"Come, my little Romeo," Vueve said, "I know you hunger to see me, hope to awaken our memories together. Soon, my love, soon."

He nodded, but tightened the grip on his blade.

Just in case—for many reasons.

And not just because the grinding sound that erupted the moment they stepped into the darkness.

The crash of the maw closing behind him.

Another slim arm wrapped around his bare chest. Slim but strong.

"Now my little Romeo," she said, "protect me from the horrors beyond, and I shall guide us to safety."

The inhumanly shrill howls that came at them suddenly.

The chills racking his whole body. Chills colder than any winter chore outside. Colder than any blizzard. Any iced over spring bath.

When suddenly his whole back was warmed by ... by ... a soft cozy feminine body pressing against it.

Rubbing his whole back with her slim belly and amply buxom chest, her nipples tracing lines up and down, up and down, over his shoulder blades, warming not just his back, but his cheeks, his head, and even the rest of his body.

As if she was a hot cocoa heating away the blizzard's cold.

"There," she said, "do not fear, or else we both shall be lost. They'll prey on our fears. That's the first form of their attack. But a sword master like you is strong in both body and mind so let's pierce through and—"

Another scream. One that drowned out all sound and thought.

One so loud it tensed Vueve enough to tighten her grip badly. Painfully bad.

Tremble even.

Romeo raised his blade—but without an obvious target he dared not strike out—yet.

Vueve gasped in his ear. Her breath. No sound reached him. Her words. Drowned out.

But she nudged him forward. Shoving him gently with her ample soft chest, and he gave way just as gently, confidently, his heart racing, but refusing to chill over.

Their pace. Faster. And faster.

His skin. Wetter. And wetter.

Her grip. Tighter. And tighter.

When the scream suddenly ended.

And the silence—worse than any scream.

For not even his racing heart made a sound.

Or all the breath blowing into his ear.

CHAPTER 23
VIVIAN

As much as her savage blade loathed it, as much as it tried to scold her hand and quiver in impotent rage, Vivian finally finished slicing this red jerkin into a crude miniskirt and high neck for Azura, despite it being crazy awful tight on her. So tight it had to be sliced in a few extra spots to make room.

No doubt pleasing Romeo to an even stupider degree.

Thank everything good that this tree trunk was so wide and big. Both Vivian and Azura could easy hid behind it with plenty of room to spare. No hiding of how much Vivian struggled to make the slices just right, here and there, and give Azura enough space to breath, to move.

Braiding the stems of the ferns together was a good idea from Azura too. She wasn't as airheaded as she came across, at least when she wasn't too panicked.

To think another girl played the airhead when she really wasn't ... he-he.

And there were still plenty of ferns around. Even if she cut down enough to give them a circle of space to work freely in.

But the soil was so dark and earthy, a single fall, a single drop and anything that touched the ground would get filthier than it already was.

The bleeding fern stems didn't help.

Too bad they couldn't get a leotard for Azura like they had for all the clawgirls. Why the demihumans had clothing that didn't recover ... strange. And Azura had such a nice outfit too ...

Once Azura was up and confident again, well, confident enough, compared to her usual self, Vivian called out for Romeo, but the silence of the forest ... *shutter*.

Really.

Shutter.

Not even single bird. No little critters either. Nothing for the lesser monsters to chow down on. It wasn't like there were a lot of pretty girls for them to feast on out in the middle of nowhere.

She would know. As a little worming, she hunted alone and with a pack. So few humans ended up deep in the woods, but enough did that, yum yum. Human flesh wasn't that bad but ever since she went honey heart resort girl—nope.

No human flesh anymore.

The few that did end up in the forest back then ... lucky for her she was mistaken for a real human girl by some regular hunters back when she was alone and lost and couldn't find a cave to hind in, but well, the rest was history.

Good history—until now.

Now that Romeo fucked her brains out, and wow, did she want it. Her legs still kinda trembled, but the attack before help her forget for a bit. Sure, it was another clawgirl's turn now and and and …

Maybe she could team up with Juliet and they'd do a threesome with Romeo sooner rather than later.

Azura and her blue bunny ears flopped low and so adorably cute, even as she pouted.

And whispered.

"I so know what you're thinking."

"The sex was … funnier than you thought, right?"

Azura giggled. "Yup!"

"If only that perverted technique …"

"Yeah … maybe …" Azura said, "can't you come up with … you know, a technique that does the same, but to him?"

"I so like know," Vivian said, "but I'm not sure he'd mind it as much."

"So?" Azura giggled, her cheeks blushed redder and redder.

"Yeah. Maybe … I don't know. *Yet.*"

Silence. Both of them.

But they both shared a cute smile.

"If only my hammer …" Azura said, "but I can't blow his clothes off without hurting him."

"I—"

Vivian gasped. The smell of brimstone was so suddenly strong.

Even Azura froze. Then cried.

"Another? How many baelzog are theeeeeeeere!"

"Just two. Now that you killed my ex and his bestie."

Behind them?!

Vivian and Azura both yelped. Turned toward their mutual enemy. Weapons up and ready and ...

Paces away, roasting away ferns in a circle around her—another pretty girl? Kinda like Velvet, but made of ash and smoke. With bright beautiful ruby eyes and long smoky dark hair. Even in an amber leotard of flame. Her hands ... like a clawgirl, but again, like ash and smoke.

Her dark lips smiled?

"Serve me again, and all will be forgiven."

Vivian didn't dignify that with a response.

But Azura shook so badly ...

"No ... nonono ... never! Slaved again? Never! Romeo is ours! Not yours!"

"Ooo," the baelzog girl said, "His name is Romeo. Cute. But I made both of you, I can unmake you both too."

Vivian hissed. Very clawgirl style.

Raised her blade.

"Then go join your exes," Vivian said, "Since—"

But the baelzog girl laughed so velvety smooth it disturbed Vivian to no end.

"I hated them more than you, Vivian," she said.

"How did you know ..."

That smirk ...

"Like I said, I made you, I can unmake you."

"That's not—"

"You clawgirls are all a part of me, understand?"

"But—"

"Now lower your weapons. Your maker and master, Lady Gryllmore insists."

For once, deep down, Vivian felt cold drenching fear. At a fate even worse than what that necromancer threatened.

A fate not even Romeo could save either of them from.

Since her limbs ... they were moving on their own.

Lowering the blade.

And the blade refused to help her resist.

Using me to cut clothing? Clothing? Let this monster consume you and I'll find a better master than that.

Vivian gulped. "I ..."

"You exist to serve me. Nothing more. **Understand?**"

Her whole body trembled. As much as Azura was trembling?

No.

More.

But Vivian, her head ... it nodded, and without her telling it to.

"And I cant' let that boy with his dangerous technique see me ... yet, can I?"

Vivian couldn't stop shaking her head.

When a howl rang out. So loud. So gut shaking—no, whole body shaking loud. A wolf howl but no chance that was a wolf.

"Ooo," the baelzog girl said, "My other creation is coming.

Time to help it do its duty. Unlike you two thought you were doing but ..."

That sinister grin of hers ...

"I think a little fusion in is order," the baelzog girl said, "or else I can't enjoy the boy before I kill him."

Moments and screams later ... Vivian and Azura, their bodies, together, and their minds, like feathers floating above a storm of flames.

Soon to be roasted to nothingness, and yet held save and sound above, like hostages.

Because now, they were almost back to where their kind had come, and deep down Vivian knew her fate, Azura's fate, worse than that necromancer planned.

They would soon be one and the same as Lady Gryllmore.

And Lady Gryllmore had a pink-haired, blue-eared bunnified clawgirl body to die for.

And soon, Romeo would die for it too.

CHAPTER 24
ROMEO

With sight and sound gone, surrounded by silent dank darkness, Romeo had no idea how long, but the smell of lemonade was overpowering and yet so sugary sweet his heart raced ever faster, and yet so calming, as if he was back in that lemonade shop and he was wasting too much of his coin on that sugary bliss.

Yet the soft warmth of Vueve Noir and her chest hugging his bare back, her presence was as solid as the cold dank stone beneath his feet. The solid dank stone to his sides. Within arms' reach. Jagged yet smooth, with sharp points everywhere, and yet his arms weren't ripped open.

Yet.

Stepping forward, he held his breath, breathing slow but steady but shallow, ready to step into a wall, or worse, off the pathway into some endless abyss.

Trust his nose, Uncle Jethron would say, but Romeo

couldn't make out anything beyond that sweet lemonade and underlying dank cave smells.

But yet Vueve nudged Romeo onward, with her chest foremost, and her nudges warmed him in more ways than one.

Nudges that made sure he didn't stop.

Didn't get lost in.

His blade. In front of him.

Ready.

Yet nothing attacked. No hint of a coming attack either.

His legs wanted to tremble. Shiver from more than the sudden cold.

But no.

His dwarven blood refused to show fear. Act on it. Especially act stupidly on it. Bad enough he acted stupid from lust, but at least understandable, given his human blood.

But fear?

Showing it?

Never!

No matter how deep, how endless this dank darkness was. How he kept creeping onward slowly but steadily.

If this was a dime dreadful, they'd soon be ambushed.

Or Vueve would betray him.

His heart pounded hard but silently. Not a sound. His ears worthless. Only feeling warm breath after breath from Vueve.

But nothing else.

Unless ... was Vueve the danger here? Maybe ... no.

Why wait so long? Why the elaborate game? No. Too elaborate. Outright stupid elaborate. That was just paranoid stupidity from fear. Unworthy of a guy with dwarven blood.

His eyes, with his dwarven blood, yeah, like gramps taught him time and time again—in pitch darkness, especially pitch darkness underground, but even at night.

Dwarven sight was the best.

Better than any mere human. His human blood wouldn't completely overwhelm it either.

Unless he let it.

And so far, Romeo had to be letting it.

He just had to be.

He took a deeeeeep, caaaalming, breath. Let himself focus on the pounding in his chest. The silent beat. A silent song.

Not on the warm chest cushioning his back. Giving his shoulder blades the sweetest rubbing of a lifetime. As sweet as the lemonade—no, no, and *no*!

His heart. The beat. Silent.

But steady.

Fast.

Yet firm. Powerful.

Not afraid, but determined. His legs wobbled with excitement, not fear. With anticipation, not cowardice. His gut clenched with hope, not lust.

Before him dark stone started to take shape. Like shadows drifting away. Becoming lighter and lighter.

Yet not a hint of more light came.

The walls, they were even more jagged and sharp and sheer as he imagined. So sharp the wetness over his arms ... not all sweat.

But the pain ... no, the sweet lemonade smell must do more than just make his mind go lustful stupid.

The pathway was narrow but straight. Like the tip of a quill scratched a straight line through the rock, and then something ravaged the sides.

But the ceiling ... vast. Dark pitch vastness.

No sign of anything above him.

No ground.

Not light.

Nothing.

Until a glowing web appeared. A giant spider web? Well above him. And as green as the steamed lima beans Aunt Tilda would punish Romeo with as dinner whenever she caught him reading a dime dreadful meant for the patrons.

Romeo held back a gasp. Turned it to a gulp.

"Veuve ..."

But stopped. He couldn't hear her answer. Just more warmth breath over his ear.

Just more utter silence.

And another web appeared. Glowing a bright ruby red. Its threads as thick as his own fingers.

Its smell ... both cherry and cobweb?

Weird ... since when did a spider web smell of cherry anything? Was it really from the spider web?

But Uncle Jethron always said trust his nose, and sniff, sniff, upward and, yeah, cherry-scented spider web.

Even weirder.

Then a glowing blue spider web appeared. Clearly

clinging to the rock above his head. Only inches from his forehead actually.

Its threads as thick as his wrists. Its smell ... sniff, sniff, blueberries?

Really?

Vueve nudged him onward. Raising his head a bit too. As if she aimed to get his eyes pressed across the thick glowing thread.

He hesitated for a moment. Nudged her hand.

Motioning for her to notice the web ahead.

But a kiss to his beck, wet and warm and sweet, and another urge onward ... sigh.

He trusted Veuve so far and didn't regret it one bit.

A dwarf didn't sway in the breeze when it came to allies and friends. Never.

So Romeo pecked the hand over his mouth, and followed the lead Veuve was urging him on to.

Let the blue web get brighter and brighter as it got closer and closer.

Let the blue spider web pressed right across both his eyes.

And passed through them?

Wow.

Romeo pecked the hand over his mouth again. Give Vueve extra credit for this neat trick.

A trick she repeated with a bright pink web. One that spanned the whole path, his whole torso, including his head.

And again for a violet spider web. One that barred a triangular cut of the path. So Vueve had turned his head jut right.

Ensured both his eyes pressed into the right threat at the right moment.

When suddenly the path was clogged with colorful spider webs. A hodgepodge of glowing bright webs. Like a twisted distorted rainbow all balled and messed up. Thick and so few gaps that ...

Veuve gave Romeo a gentle hug—and nudged him forward.

Even faster than before.

Almost too fast to react in time.

Almost ... until it was.

CHAPTER 25
JULIET

Juliet tried her best not to grumble, or grumble as silently as she could, but jumping to twisting branch to twisting branch for so long was tiring her out.

But as crisp and musty as the dank air was up here ...

As frightfully annoying as the sparrows were whenever she passed through another flock of them ...

She didn't stop.

No.

She dashed faster and faster. As fast as Velvet was, judging by the tap-tap-tap from the branch right beside her.

As heart-pounding fun as going battle bitch cricket was sometimes ... well ... she really wasn't looking forward to the coming battle.

Or leaving Romeo behind with that spider girl bitch.

No telling what other monsters were out here. Ready to lure and—ack!

Juliet almost slipped. Almost fell right on her ass.

But she gnashed her teeth, shook her head, and slapped her cheeks together.

"Get it together, Juliet."

Romeo needed her to get through this craziness. To save him from that spider girl like he saved her from the necromancer days ago.

Maybe she'd even get to embarrass him like he embarrassed her.

The very thought, she was smiling before she knew it.

But no time for pleasure—yet. The thick canopy blocked too much of her ordinary vision. Her other vision, she hadn't used it since forever, and it could strain her eyes badly if she overused it, especially when she was tired, but ...

Velvet giggled close by.

"No serpent vision yet?"

"No ... it hurts my eyes if—"

"Aaaah, you're doing it wrong."

"Wrong? Then how ..." Juliet perked up. "there's a right way?!"

"Yes, of course, you—hush!"

"Hush? How—"

"Quiet now. Something's—"

Another wolfish howl, then shrill scream, like her own dragon father furious and hungry same time.

This time further away? As if it was headed away from them. As if it was afraid.

Good.

Better it was afraid. It should be.

Juliet and Velvet weren't exactly push-overs. Not anymore. Least Juliet wasn't. Velvet probably never was.

And least it was still in front of them. Sort of.

Another wolf howl. Form further ahead o them. One that turned into another scream, but not reptilian?

No.

More like a boy's scream?

"What the ..." Juliet said. "Velvet do we ..."

"Demihuman, I think," Velvet said, "No doubt another enemy."

Velvet even chuckled sinister. "Maybe one less enemy now."

"Yeah," Juliet still felt chilled. "Let's hope."

They both dashed onward. Juliet following the beat of her own heart. Leap. Leap. Leap. Like some grasshopper again. So natural and yet so odd.

Until another howl. Very close. Below them, almost.

Then a boy's scream.

The same boy?

"Please! Help! Someone!"

An icy touch streaked down her spine, but Juliet said, "Let's help. I ..."

"Helping an enemy," Velvet said, "Could get us killed. Or worse, but ..."

"But what?"

Velvet giggled so sultry sweet and happy?

"A little competition for Romeo," Velvet said, "might set him straight too."

Juliet huffed.

Then smiled.

"Yeah, *exactly*."

CHAPTER 26

KROTHA RIGOT

Despite chanting all the right chants.

Despite pressing the boy's awful blade as the perfect sacrifice.

Despite her core being as demonic black as the very core before her ...

Nothing.

Nothing she was doing sparked life in her masters.

As if this dark dank hole was their grave, not their prison, but that ... that's impossible!

The boy's blade wasn't the only sacrificial blade she had in her possession. That strange other blade held by that traitorous wolf man. A wolf man now spored so completely and utterly he had followed her down here as if obeying her unconscious will, a will to help her and only her.

Right behind her. Along the path. In total darkness.

In total silence.

The towering high wolf man already offered his magnificent blade to awaken their true masters and ... he even kneeled!

Perfect.

Maybe he would serve as a better mount than this fox.

But extracting herself from this fox would take time she didn't have. So not yet.

But soon.

First Krotha chanted the perfectly correct chants.

Pressed both enchanted blades into the core.

Offered all her power and more to this magnificent demonic core of her masters.

Over and over and over again.

Yet nothing.

Krotha wailed. So close and yet so far. No!

Do not despair. That was for her enemies to do. Not her.

Again she tried, but this time she dared to the unthinkable.

She offered her own demonic core as part of the sacrifice.

Touching hers with theirs.

And ...

And ...

!

The cores fused. The giant demonic core of her masters fused into her smaller core. Making it darker than anything she could have ever imagined.

Ever.

Her power ... beyond imagining. Vengeance for her clan would not be enough now.

Never.

With this power ... she could break the world.

Remake it so that her clan lived once again.

Her beloved mate would return.

Her clan, her mate for the mere sacrifice of the right human boy and right clawgirl.

Romeo Bladell and his wretched Juliet.

For the instant and final death of their whole entire wretched races.

A worthy sacrifice.

And a reward for her devotion.

The age of men would end.

And the age of the hobgobble would begin.

CHAPTER 27
ROMEO

Romeo couldn't even gasp at what he saw next.

Blink. Blink. Blink.

Just the smells, full of cobweb but yet also a fruit cocktail of sweet delights. The juiciest kind of fruit salads only the best of the best patrons got at the Honey Heart Resort, and never any leftovers for him.

Just the smell cooled the wave of heat washing over him. It was the kind of heat the hovered over the hottest rock on the hottest days of summer. The kind of heat that begged for a dip into a cool spring.

Yet the sight ... like a brilliantly colorful fruit salad formed of highly detailed berry-style webs and stems of slightly darker but harder looking webbing.

No sign of the walls, but the bright glow of all the colorful webs ... wow.

Just ... wow.

No sign of the sky either. Just more webbing woven like gigantic fruits doubling as hanging homes, judging by the openings and hanging walkways between the openings.

A city of webs.

Webs woven like yummy, yummy fruit.

Wow.

And so many round fruits that the breeze hitting him from above ... from underneath all that fruity yummy smells, wow, there was a strong hint of musty earthy forest.

Maybe ... the city was below ground, probably, but the top was open to Shadow Forest?

Maybe?

Aunt Tilda would just love this kind of place for patrons. No doubt if she ever saw it she'd seek out a way to imitate it, even just a little bit.

No wonder pa and ma went out adventuring, even if they never came back, seeing sights like this ... amazing!

Even if Aunt Tilda would be furious he left without saying a word.

Without sending word.

Forget the supplies themselves ... he left them safe and sound in a tree he could easily find again—as long as he retraced his way back into Shadow Forest.

The floor itself here was ... dark stone like the cave he was just in, but from the glow of all the colorful webbing, wow, it was like an exotic painting of abstract art only the best of the best artist could hope to imitate.

The hanging fruit homes even swayed slightly in the downward breeze.

Yet not a sound—yet.

Nothing.

The hand over his mouth, Veuve's hand, he gave her a gentle squeeze.

But this time she guided him around. Let him face her, finally, and Holy Mother of the Flame Moon was she gorgeous.

The very sight of her, the smell of her, like a cool lemonade during a blazing summer drought.

With shoulder-length wedges of sunny hair, and ruby red locks framing a slim pixie pretty face with the most gorgeous and glowing bright green eyes beaming so proud and happy at him and only him ...

Vueve fluttered her ... butterfly wings? Wow. Was she a fairy of some sort? Black swallowtail wings with red bucktail patterns.

That breeze from them ... yes, that lemonade scent was very much from her.

Romeo gulped. Heart pounding and he could hear again!

"Vueve ..."

Vueve took such a deep nervous breath, and yet clearly stumbled from him gazing into her lush green eyes.

Maybe he could give her a look down and up? Break the eye contact and give her a moment to recover?

Her high neck minidress was so beautifully it sheened in the colorful light, and yet it fit snuggly over her amazing slim yet curved figure that—ack!

She jumped forward, kissed him so deep and passion-ately, his shock at her passion, her action, made him stumble just as much as she had, but her passion was no doubt as deep as his attraction to her.

She even pressed her chest, an ample buxom chest comparable even to Juliet's, and then the rest of her, supple and smooth, and he hugged her back, embracing her passion, feeling up her dress, a dress as smooth and lovely as the best kind of silk.

The kind of silk dress any Honey Heart girl would kill to have.

Suddenly his pants ... down? his legs cool, yet warming up?

And Vueve ... her dress ... ah! Gone. Off. Her body. Bare body was against his own. Warming each other. Cuddling Rubbing passionate.

Her bare nipples rubbing against his bare chest. Her legs hugging against his.

Romeo entered her. Plunging in. Like a dip in the perfect hot spring.

Their gasps, pants, and moans of passion, of relief ...

He released his own hot spring within her, and her scream of bliss matched his own.

Even when countless girly giggles came from high above them.

CHAPTER 28
JULIET

Juliet gasped at the sight below.

A dozen paces below the twisting branches full of oh-so-slippery moss and tons of hiding chirpy sparrows was a small round clearing.

The ground itself was like a broken shattered floor—kinda like whenever Romeo had to fix a lot of stuff underneath her own bedroom floor—but here, it was from lots of shattered boulders, not ruined floor boards.

The very smell was earthy and murky and yet very chalky. Like the boulders were shattered very recently.

But Juliet and Velvet would have heard it, right?

Yeah.

The fine mist overhanging the place, like a cloud of chalk, and she used plenty of chalk in those games he used to play with Romeo and ... no.

It was murkier than the abandoned wells she and her pack, back as wormlings, often forged from.

Even going so far as to hunt the scary creatures lurking in their depths.

As spooky scary as that was—they knew they could be scarier.

They had to be.

Jut like now. Juliet and Velvet would be scarier than any of their enemies.

Or all of them combined.

But her regular sight couldn't make out any enemies below. Or even the source of the howls or screams from before.

Too many of the boulders had overhangs. Hiding whatever was down below in shadows and mats of overhanging moss tangled with thick craggy roots.

The chalky cloud wasn't helping either.

Juliet had her scimitars together in a bow. Ready to bolt dead any threat that dared rear its ugly head.

Or—a moment later—a very handsome head.

On a very Tall, Dark, and Handsome wolf boy.

Gulp.

That kind that made a girl's legs tremble for all the best reasons. His wolf ears and tail were only chocolate frosting on that chocolate beefcake of yummy. Strapped in only snug pants. His broad muscular chest rippled with just the right amount of fuzzy hair.

Just like his chiseled perfect face.

He was right below her. Had Juliet been wearing a skirt, and he looked, he could have—no!

Juliet was in this creepy leotard, phew!

But Romeo would *soooo* jealous if she ... she ... no!

She refused to cheat on Romeo. The only reason Romeo even went harem on her with her packmates was they had all agreed on it.

That she had gotten herself captured that first day.

Certain she had to be killed with her new packmates, but no. Romeo saved them all.

Even if it was an a rather perverted way.

Juliet gulped again.

But if Romeo could harem some girls, why couldn't Juliet even ogle another guy? Not fair.

Not fair at all.

From a branch right beside Juliet, Velvet hissed quietly.

"Too handsome to harm—so watch out."

Juliet nodded.

Gulped.

"If only we were too cute to kill, right?"

"If only—but don't count on it."

"I know."

Velvet had her scimitars snapped together in bow form too. Aimed at the wolf boy.

At his heart.

But her face was stretched in an uneasy grimace.

Juliet did to but ...

"If he's undead—"

"Too bad for girlkind."

With a stern grimace the handsome dream of a wolf boy motioned with his hands?

Beside the first wolf boy, another wolf boy came out. A Tall, Blond, and All-Too-Handsome wolf boy? Since when did such cute boys get together in packs?

His chiseled but dainty expression, along with more bare broad chest with right the right amount of hair, and all a lovey golden blonde ... gulp.

Really.

Gulp.

Too cute to kill was right, but ...

If only Romeo was here, and not with that tramp of a spider girl—

Suddenly the Tall, Dark, and Handsome wolf boy took a deep stern breath.

"Velvet Ruins?"

His voice was like chocolate made into sound.

Velvet hissed.

"Dendre? Which side? Quickly. Or elsssse ..."

She pulled the purple bolt in her bow back even further.

With another deep but quiet breath, the Tall, Dark, and Handsome Dendre placed his big firm hands on his waist, and stayed all too calm and patient as he looked up at Velvet.

Not one bit of fear.

"Whichever side you're on, and I heard it's no longer with Macker and his crew."

Velvet gulped loud, and all-too-clear.

"I found a mate. A new pack. It'ssss …"

"Good for you," Dendre said, "but you're still hissing like a little worming."

The other Tall, Blond, and All-Too-Handsome boy sighed, shaking his head.

"A mate you haven't mated with. A shame. Real shame."

"Hush! He … there's a whole pack he must mate with. One at a time. And I'm patient. Far more patient than you, Bellon."

"Too patient," that blonde Bellon said, "or maybe too reluctant?"

Why did they have to be such assholes? Juliet growled, and didn't let up on her ready bolt.

"Velvet is next," Juliet said, "Once we … well … why do you care?!"

Both Dendre and Bellon sighed. Rolled their eyes at Velvet, and at Juliet.

Velvet gulped.

"Wait. I didn't tell them … yet. There hasn't been time. Really."

This time Juliet gulped.

"Told us what?"

Dendre grimaced at Juliet?

"Should I tell her or …"

Velvet gasped.

"No! I'll tell them. Soon. Jussssst, well …"

Bellon huffed fiercely. Smacked his fist into his palm.

"If that bastard mistreated you, we'll kill him and—"

Juliet yelped.

"No! it's not like that. Really. Velvet, what's going on? Are they friends? Then why ..."

"It's ... complicated."

Dendre and Bellon glanced at each other.

Dendre grumbled.

"Complicated?"

Then Bellon grumbled.

"So she says."

Juliet pouted fiercely at the lot of them.

"And that creature that howled and screamed and ..."

Now, with another loud huff, Dendre folded his arms over his massive chest, and so sexy enough to make Juliet almost gulped for the best kind of wrongest reason.

The forest was all too silent now. Not a hint of that howling screaming thing now.

And Juliet was start to trembled from crouching too long on this low branch.

Velvet grumbled, more like moaned a whimpered, but it was Bellon that answered, finally, and his voice was a lot like lemonade on a hot day.

"We dealt with it. A few bolts from you lovely girls wouldn't have been enough to throw it off for long."

Juliet huffed, but with relief.

"Really? Then ..."

Juliet snapped her bow back into scimitars and—

"Juliet!" Velvet said, "Wait!"

"But ..."

Both handsome wolf boys chuckled, but not sinisterly,

not at all, so Juliet pouted at Velvet, and sheathed her scimitars.

An instant later a massive hand engulfed her head.

Yanked her head back. Neck bare and ready to snap.

Or slice open.

"Drop your bow, Velvet," Bellon said, "Your little rebellion is over."

CHAPTER 29
ROMEO

Holding the gorgeous Veuve in one arm, and holding her warm and cuddling close to his own bare naked body, Romeo smiled up at the countlessly giggling girls hidden within the hanging homes of fruit-shaped webbing.

The sway of the hanging fruit homes was even more pronounced. As obvious as the countless girl giggles clearly savoring the sight of him ... going at it so passionately with Vueve.

And still ready to go passionately with her again.

In fact, the stone beneath his feet wasn't cold or dank. It was nice and warm. Felt clean and cozy, in fact, so ...

Maybe ...

With a giggle, Veuve stroked his chest with her forefinger and then kissed him again so passionately, tugging him down onto the ground

There was no doubt what she wanted next.

More like how she wanted to fuck him next.

Back to the flat warm stone, Romeo held her lust hips over his. Let her ride him like her wettest dream of a stallion come true. Her cries of joy, pants of passion, she slipped his hands over the curves of her side.

Soft supple curves.

And onto her breasts. Pressing them deep and firm. Grabbing them. As she screamed sultry sexy and rode him even faster, more passionately, like this race was the most critical in her life, like he'd be hers and hers alone if she won it, and winning it she was.

Even as he burst another hot spring of seed into her.

And she fell down beside him. Moaning happy and pleased, as she rubbed against his side, embracing him as much as he embraced her.

Romeo whispered, "Vueve ..."

"Oh my lovely Romeo, hush ... the wait ..."

"Worth it."

She giggled. "I know."

And Vueve kissed him passionately again.

Letting him roll over her. On top of her. Spreading her legs and once more embraced him, but with those fantastic curved sexy legs of her.

This time he rode her, and wow, she did soar, despite not moving from the spot. her pants and moans were so passionate, so wonderfully orgasmic, he released another hot spring of seed into her, just as she rolled them onto their side.

Kissed him again.

"Oh my lovely Romeo," Vueve said, "Your naughty harem is in danger, but if you trust me, maybe we can still save them."

That jolted him.

Like a sudden dip into ice water.

Almost shriveled parts of a guy that a guy didn't want shriveled.

Almost.

"I trust you," Romeo said, and kissed Vueve passionately on her lips again, as if his intense passion could prove it.

Vueve hugged him around his neck.

"Oh my sweet lovely Romeo," she said, ""how I wish we could do this all day and night, but alas—"

A haughty and clearly annoyed huff came from right above them both.

The stink of serpent. Of dragon.

"What do we have here?"

That voice, a familiar dragon voice—Juliet's dad's voice, and from right above them?

Oh crap.

They were so eaten it wasn't funny.

CHAPTER 30
ROMEO

Back dressed as best he could, in only slacks and boots now, Romeo was very much not eaten—yet.

But only for now.

(Probably.)

His ass was very much still rooted to the warm stone floor. The flood of beautiful colors around him a small relief to the nightmare he knew he was soon going to face.

That the hanging fruit homes were swaying only slightly faster ... no chance a dragon of that size could have squeezed through. Not at all.

There had to be another way here.

Never mind Juliet's father wasn't blasting them both with deadly hot flame—yet.

Thankfully Fleur and Claudia were also near Romeo. Behind him, actually, so no death by fire yet, probably.

Even if Vueve and her gorgeous ass was right beside him,

hugging his side as firmly. As firmly as the brightly lit stone pressed against both of their asses. It was as if she was determined to meet her end if Romeo did.

And honestly, part of him liked that kind of crazy about her.

And it was kind of crazy, come to think about it. They did just met and yet they already went full-blown passionate lovers ...

So quickly and yet—

The dragon tsked loud and scornful.

"What part of no-sex-still-safe didn't you understand, **boy**?"

Vueve pouted so fiercely and yet so determined.

"This is my home," Vueve said, "it's as safe as—"

"Oh," the dragon said, "don't worry, I'll get to you next. But for now—"

"My lovely Romeo is *mine* to—"

"Next means next, **girl**."

That a little flame popped out of his nostrils, and heated up the place badly despite it being seeming to be so little ... Vueve thankfully only huffed, but stayed silent now.

The giggled above them all, from the countless webbed homes ... somehow Romeo sensed they wouldn't come to their rescue either.

Not when that flame could easily destroy their entire webbed village.

And no telling how far this dragon would go to make a point.

Especially now.

Romeo grimaced, but held back a harsh fearful gulp.

"That was between my clawgirl harem and me," Romeo said, "not Vueve. She—"

"She reminds me of what Juliet might have become," the dragon said, "had not fate separated us so early."

Um ... phew?

"Don't blame Vueve," Romeo said, "She didn't even know about the no-sex-till-safe thing."

"Something you should have mentioned sooner, ey?"

Now Romeo pouted.

"Since we all might end up dying," he said, "some sex *before*—"

The dragon burst out laughing.

"Before you get yourselves killed?" he said, "Better no sex so that none of you get yourselves killed. That foolish lusting is already distracting the two of you beyond—"

Vueve grumbled loud and annoyed. She even pounded the stone solidly with her fist.

"I'm in season! And this is the first time I've had a mate! I only have so many seasons and and and ... if there's war coming ... no, not if, *when* ... I don't want to die a virgin. That's ... embarrassing. You'd never understand. It's ..."

"Oh really?" the dragon said, "I'll have you know Juliet's mother and I didn't start out as companions. More like enemies. And quite a fight it was! That she was a virgin and begged me to at least deflower her *before* finishing her off ... well ... as strange as that might sound ... one thing led to another and she very much ended up surviving."

Romeo ... knew better than to say anything ... about that.

He felt Vueve cringing, but she clearly hid it by hugging into him, and he helped by hugging her back.

"So what you're saying ..." Vueve said, "is that I should have stayed a virgin so I could beg to be deflowered by whoever defeated me—assuming it was some guy who got me. Really?"

"That's not what I meant," the dragon said.

"But that's what you said!"

"Now look here daughter," the dragon said, "I—"

Romeo gasped.

"How many daughters do you have?"

That ... oh crap. The dragon did NOT look happy about that question.

"Apparently not enough," the dragon said, "since you seem intent on hareming every single daughter I sired."

Vueve gasped now.

"Wait ..." she said, "how many sisters do I have? I know about Fleur and Juliet, and Velvet, but ..."

Romeo flinched.

"Fleur ... you're Juliet's sister? I thought you and Claudia ..."

Claudia sighed right behind Vueve.

"We're half-sisters, not full-blood sisters."

Fleur rubbed Romeo's head. Soft and warmly, but very very awkwardly.

"I-I-I ... yesssss. We're ... you know. Ssssame mother, different father. So ..."

"Hey!" Claudia said, "Since when did you go nervous mouse girl again?"

"S-s-sorry," Fleur said, "I'm next, b-b-b-but …"

"I know," Claudia said, "but your father here seems intent on scaring—"

"V-V-Velvet will," Fleur said, "get him n-n-next. I know it, no?"

Romeo sighed, dejection clearly showing.

"At this rate—"

The dragon puffed out a loud bit of flaming smoke. Heating up the whole place a bit far too much.

"Yes, yes," the dragon said, "Juliet, Velvet, and Fleur are my clawgirl daughters. You, Vueve Noir are my archnofey daughter. And there's that ditzy but pretty bunny girl Azura who's my demihuman daughter. There. That's all I know about, and clearly this Romeo has now claimed them all as his mates, and *more*!"

Claudia groaned.

"Better mates than bounties."

"Well …" the dragon said.

"And Juliet would have given him an amazing bounty."

"Yes, but …"

"Fleur and Velvet too. Stunningly great bounties. Not to mention myself."

"True, but …"

"Especially Azura. Proving that there's hostile demihumans? Best bounty of all."

"Of course, of course, but …"

"Some sex *now*," Claudia said, "to cement the whole mates for life thing, when, you know, he's up and eager to fuck us plenty and more, sounds pretty good to me. Too many guys would fuck us and then try snagging the bounty. Let alone all the guys that would skip the fucking."

"Well ... true ..."

"Exactly. He's been protecting us. As best he can. Far better than most guys even would consider trying. So stop pestering him about—"

"I'm not pestering him," the dragon said, "I'm—"

"Being far too overprotective," Claudia said, "in the *wrong* way."

"Well ... I'm their father!" the dragon said, "Of course I'm not exactly keen on them *all* having the same guy, a guy they just met, and then ... then ..."

Boom. In the distance.

Loud enough to shake all the webbing above the dragon, from the fruit homes, to the walkways between them, and violently.

Fearful whimpers came from the homes.

No archnofey showed herself—yet.

The dragon growled.

"**Boy**," he said, "where's your sword?"

Romeo gulped. Chills racking his body, despite the warmth from Vueve against him, and Fleur so close to him too.

"I ... I haven't recovered it yet."

The dragon tsked. His expression even fiercer now.

"You'll need a weapon, and quickly. A good weapon. Not that crummy wooden blade you dropped back there before you started ... my daughter."

"Where?"

Vueve jumped to her feet.

"I know! There's a blade we keep hidden, deep just for this kind of moment!"

More fearful murmurs came from above them, but clearly none dared show themselves yet.

Protest whatever was happening too much.

So far.

Maybe this dragon scared them too, and they knew better than to make themselves even bigger targets.

For now. But later ... after the dragon left ...

The dragon huffed and tsked again, sending more flaming smoke out of his nostrils.

"You mean the Fairy Blade of Ravaging, ey?"

Vueve folded her arms over her chest.

"Yup! And you—"

"Approve whole heartedly."

Silence?

Something was off, and big time.

Vueve gasped. Finally. The first sound.

"You ... approve?"

"Of course," the dragon said, "if this brat survives, a **very big** IF, I would say, then—"

Vueve yanked Romeo to his feet. Bounced excited in place that some of her energy was exciting him as well.

"Did you hear that?! Father will approve of us, of you, once you win that blade!"

Romeo nodded. Gave the dragon another look.

"No more of this—"

"Of course, of course now. Prove worthy of that blade and

you can enjoy the loins of my daughters, and their friends, as much as you desire. But better hurry. Not much time left, ey?"

"Time left?"

The dragon chuckled.

"To enter the tournament. A combat tournament. The blade you seek was already stolen from this village and will be given to the winner of the tournament in that village by your home ... what's it called ..."

It wasn't just Vueve that gasped ...

Romeo gulped too.

"Then ... how ... do we get there."

"Bring my daughters Velvet and Juliet with you," the dragon said, "and I'll fly you over. But you better hurry. Auditions will begin within the hour and you know how late comers get treated ..."

Romeo nodded. Heart sinking deeper than any abyss.

CHAPTER 31

MACKER THE CRUEL

Macker the Cruel raised up from his knees. The smell of ashy slog long gone. The breeze finally dared to stir up once more.

Craters remained where his knees dug deep into the dark soil. Shards of boulders where his fists rampaged down in grief.

And he wasn't alone.

All the ferns, trees, and boulders ... all destroyed. Ravaged. Savaged. Now just wreckage. Worthless wreckage.

A whole field of wreckage. His demihuman warriors had eyes red with grief. Whether living or undead.

All his hobgobbles, whether big or small, but all now undead, they all still drooled the green watery goo of grief from their massive maws.

But no clawgirls were here to honor their former masters.

No.

Those traitors ... no. No more time for grief.

It was time for vengeance.

And—

?

In front of him, a pink-haired clawgirl with blue bunny ears. One that looked so tasty it hurt not to munch her down right this instant, but no. Something was different about this clawgirl.

Something grander.

!

Macker fell to his knees. Bowed so deep his head smashed into the ground, crushed more rocks.

"Mistress! I—"

"No need for the hysterics. Earn forgiveness by slaying the dragon that dared defy his former masters."

"Of course, my Mistress."

"Your demiwolf Captains Bellon and Dendre even captured two more renegade clawgirls. Clawgirls of the same blood as that wretched dragon, so time once again earn that cruel surname of yours."

"Oh yes! Mistress I—"

"Yes, yes, I know. With the dragon gone the archnofey village will be ours for the devastating, but my spies caught wind if something more important."

Silence.

Was Macker worthy of hearing the rest?

After failing to recognize her in this form ...

His Mistress giggled sultry sweet once again.

"Just teasing. You're worthy of this next mission. The

Fairy Blade of Ravaging. Some human in a nearby village have it. Are holding a silly tournament to determine who will lay claim to it."

"That village shall feel your vengeance! Their men shall wail in despair as their women and spawn are eaten alive and screaming before them and—"

"Love the enthusiasm but not what I had in mind—yet. We're joining the tournament. Openly. As contestants. Since it suits the perfect ritual I had in mind. A ritual that would avoid the need for a full-blown invasion. Saves us a lot of trouble and might be lots more fun."

"As you wish, My Mistress."

His Mistress giggled so sweet and happy.

"Yes. And we won't be the only ones joining the tournament as contestants ..."

Her giggles spelled doom for their enemies.

Enemies whose doom was coming.

No matter how much those pathetic worms struggled.

CHAPTER 32
ROMEO

With the wooden blade Vivian fashioned for him in his hands, Romeo now hung in that dragon's claws like a bunny caught by an overly merciful eagle.

(Or sadistic eagle.)

The wind whipped around Romeo. Smacking him around the way this dragon no doubt wanted to smack him around. The chill from being shirtless not helping either, but his dwarven blood refused to let him shiver.

A guy with dwarf blood could handle far worse and simply shrug it off. This was nothing. Just a good fast way to get somewhere.

Nothing more.

Of course, the girls got to ride the dragon properly. On his back. Safe and sound.

But not Romeo.

Well, this only meant Romeo would be ready for battle even sooner.

Ready to rescue Velvet and Juliet—assuming they needed rescuing.

A big assumption.

But down below. hundreds of paces below, the thick canopy spread out like a jagged green carpet. An expanse smelling of musty earthy horror every Honey Heart Resort patron had loved bragging about at one time or another.

Least the sky was mostly clear.

No thunder storms. Nothing. Not even a cloud. Not even a little white puff.

Just bright blue sky today.

Until an inhuman scream erupted right below them.

So loud and shocking Romeo cringed for a moment.

Only a moment.

And an almost fatal moment.

Except this dragon didn't flinch. Didn't cringe. Didn't even fly higher.

No.

The dragon diving lower,.

Faster.

Another scream erupted well ahead of them. An instant later something exploded from the canopy.

A giant green worm. Covered in moss and worse. With a toothy maw and two pairs of huge battish wings.

The smell ... too much like a slimy rotting log in a filthy swamp.

The flying worm screamed at the dragon again.

The dragon charged so fast at the worm, the worm was shocked, already scrambling to react. Decide how to catch the dragon without hurting itself badly too.

A huge puff of smoke and flame. Shielding the dragon from the worm's line of sight—or line of senses, since there were no obvious eyes ...

Another scream. The canopy exploded.

But once the flame cleared the worm was gone.

"Coward!" the dragon said, "A little game of chicken in the air and the bastard runs away. Like usual."

Okay, this dragon was crazy. A lot like his daughters. More like the other way around.

"Ah," the dragon said, "There they are, and good. They're in trouble. So **boy**, go rescue them—*now!*"

The dragon suddenly dived so low it seemed like he'd crash into the canopy.

No.

He just flung Romeo down at full speed, and called out.

"If you cant' survive that, you'd never survive that tournament!"

CHAPTER 33
ROMEO

That dragon was sadistically crazy, but first things first. Stopping this fall. And quickly.

Before Romeo was battered into a bloody pulp by the branches and cratered into the ground like a pancake smacked into a frying pan.

The canopy was too much like a thick web of solid branches and daggerish twigs and slappy leaves.

A single smack of a solid branch and he was done for. A broken arm. Or a broken leg.

Forget winning any tournament at anything less than his peak.

The twigs stabbed him everywhere. Ripped at him as he fell through the canopy. The leave slapping him even hard.

As hard as Juliet at her angriest.

And damn, she should be angry this time. He left his

harem out to fend for themselves while he followed some new beauty to his potential doom.

Only his luck proved good. So far.

Except now he was careening toward the dark solid ground. The speed of his fall so fast it gusted the air into him without breathing. And the earthy must stabbed his insides.

Good thing Romeo had this blade out and ready.

No choice either.

Let it touch a branch at this speed and it would shattered.

The twigs ripping at it were bad enough.

No. Focus on his heart. Its pounding.

The rhythm of battle.

Thump.

Thump.

Thump.

Good.

Romeo was ready to unleash his Slash-o-Boom Technique. Use its forceful impact to soften his landing.

A glimpse of sunny blonde hair?

Yeah.

In the branch above the ground. The very branch he was careening toward. Lots of sunny hair. Too much to be Juliet's.

And a broad chest. Too brawny. Too masculine for Juliet.

A massive hand. His hand. Clutching the head of ... Juliet?!?!?!?

No time!

Romeo unleashed his Slash-o-Boom Technique.

Right at the bastard clutching Juliet's head.

A grunt from the guy ... with blond wolf ears and tail? In slacks only?

A demihuman wolf guy!

And his other hand stretched out.

Caught Romeo's technique?!

The impact only forced the bastard to grunt again. His arm bending back, but only some. Ripple his broad hairy chest with effort.

Make the branch he was on creeeeeeaaaaaak with loud torment.

But Romeo wasn't done.

The force of his first Slash-o-Boom slowed his fall. Some.

But didn't change his course.

Right crash into the wolf man.

Blade plunging right through that massive chest.

Snapping.

Shattering.

The wolf man gasped. Shocked.

Utterly, utterly shocked.

While Romeo used the momentum to flip above the wolf man. Pushing the rest of his fall into the massive bastard. Swing around.

Just as the wolf man fell, Crashed down into the ground several paces below.

Boom.

As good as dead, right?

Good.

Romeo landed right behind Juliet. her head now safe and

free. She was still crouching and gasping, gagging for breath. Stumbling back in shock—until Romeo caught her. With his legs. Than hands.

"You're safe now."

"O-O-Other. More."

Huh? What!

CHAPTER 34
ROMEO

Like pa always told Romeo, keep an eye on his surroundings. It was key to keeping up an advantage.

Or losing whatever advantage he already had.

The thick craggy branch Romeo stood on, holding Juliet safely as she crouched against his legs, the moss could easily make either of them slip if he wasn't careful. If they made any jerky moves.

Most of the branches here were thick craggy and wound around each other.

Perfect for that speedy grasshopper maneuvering that Vivian loved to mess Romeo up with back during their bouts together at the Honey Heart Resort.

The few tree trunks were as wide as the gut of that dragon and bearded with lots of moss. Only jumping and carefully could get anyone from branch to branch.

Something only clawgirls could hope to manage so quickly and well.

The ground below was ... holy Flame ... several paces below all the many boulders had been smashed everywhere. Utter wreckage. Rubble. A cloud of dust. Gray and fine. From shattered rock and stone.

Just the smell ... chalkier than when Juliet when she went teacher beauty all to instruct stupid him on some critical rule thing he needed to know to play those board games with her.

In fact, Velvet in all her toasted almond glory was crouched on a branch right beside and above Juliet.

Her focus—the ground beyond Romeo and Juliet.

Purple bolts zipped passed them. From Velvet. Aimed a few paces to Romeo's side.

Below.

Another enemy!

A moan came from right below them. From that blond wolf bastard.

"Damn. That human brat almost got me too."

The blond bastard of a wolf man was already staggering up to his feet. The wooden blade protruded from his chest, above his heart.

And a bit too far to the right.

No other sign of damage? Really?

Not even a scratch from the many flying shards of wood. The smell of exploded oak. No. It wasn't just Romeo's imagination.

His wooden blade had exploded from the impact. Shattered. And yet the blond wolf man hadn't suffered any lasting damage, well, except for being impaled through the chest.

A wound that wasn't even slowing him down.

Just annoyed him.

Them came a chuckle. Not from the blond bastard, but from a black-haired wolf man now beside him. One just as broad in brawn as the blond wolf man.

"Bellon, you freak. You leaving that twig in?"

The blond wolf man named Bellon grinned sinister and blood-thirsty.

"Yeah, Dendre. For now it's a lesson. Don't lower our guard against these brats."

Juliet was shivering in Romeo's arms. More than enough to rage his heart, make it pound fierce for battle.

"R-R-Romeo. Here."

She slipped out one of her scimitars. Giving it to him again.

"You n-need it. More than me."

Romeo kissed the top of Juliet's lovely head.

"You know I love you."

"I know." She hugged his arms holding her. "And I trust you. Go kill those freaks and I'll ..."

"Stay back, and watch my back."

He pecked her lovely cheek. Warm and moist.

"Sure." Juliet giggled. "And your cute butt."

Both wolf men growled fiercer than ... than ... something, brainfart, but around the gorgeously beautiful Juliet brain-farts were the happy norm.

Still, it was Dendre that growled some words out first.

"Disgusting. A human and a clawgirl. Don't you bitches have any taste?"

It was Velvet who answered this time.

"We have excellent taste. It's you two idiots who can't land a girlfriend. And with your looks—"

Bellon huffed, smirking up at Velvet.

"Who needs a girlfriend when they'll fuck us both without any of the baggage."

Dendre laughed even more sinister.

"You're the idiot, Velvet. Ruining your own seduce and slay streak for some worthless fugly?"

"And what a fucking ugly that brat is," Bellon said, "His stink is so bad—"

A rain of purple bolts pounded down at both wolf men.

But they dodged the bolts so easily.

Far too quickly for their big brawned-up size.

Before Romeo knew it, that blond bastard Bellon was suddenly back up on their branch. A few paces beyond Romeo and yet the bastard was so heavy the whole entire branch started sinking some.

Creak loud and dangerously clear.

Romeo turned toward him. Pale blue scimitar out and ready to strike.

More violet bolts rained down on the other wolf man, Dendre.

"Their hearts," Velvet said, "strike their heart and they die. Everywhere else they'll recover and quickly."

Dendre growled. Muscles bulging and rippling even more.

"Giving away our secret," he said, "You really want to ruin our fun, don't you Velvet."

"I'm called Velvet Ruins for a reason, *boys*."

More violet bolts flew his way.

But all missed.

While Bellon marched closer.

And closer.

Only paces away, when Juliet slipped up to her feet? Back to Romeo's back.

But trembling so badly she might end up slipping on the branch's moss. Even with her back balancing her against him.

"I won't," Juliet said, "I won't be useless. Not again."

Again? She was never useless but … oh. Maybe getting caught by that necromancer a few days ago really knocked down her confidence?

"You're not useless," Romeo said, "Your talents aren't in direct combat, but … wait a moment."

"Wait? For what!"

"What about strategy and tactics? Like those board games you always beat me at?"

"Those were just games," Juliet said, "this is real. One mistake and … the rules, there aren't really any rules either. Just …"

Both wolf men chuckled even more sinister.

Bellon loomed closer and closer now too.

Started winding up his fist. As if warning both Romeo and Juliet of the obvious attack coming. Why he'd do that instead of a direct less obvious punch …

"That blonde bimbo," Bellon said, "makes us blonds look too dumb."

Then flung his fist forward. Paces too far away.

Or so it seemed.

The power of the punch flew forward.

Faster.

Smashed into Romeo. Through him.

Into Juliet. Her yelp.

Slip.

Bang.

Her crotch. The branch. She moaned. Loud and aching.

Yet somehow she managed to help Romeo steady himself. Avoid the same awful fate.

Yet their misfortune made Dendre bark a laugh. Dodging even more violet bolts even better. Even if they forced him back more and more.

Until they didn't.

A shower of violet bolts. A violent spray.

All bolts returning at Velvet.

Her yelp.

Snap.

Clang. Clang. Clang.

Scimitars deflected them all.

Barely.

For now.

CHAPTER 35
JULIET

Juliet ached too much to get up. Her legs instinctively hugged the thick branch. The moss cushioned away the worst of the fall, but that attack, she knew it, they had techniques like Romeo did, but without the need for a blade.

Her with one blade, and in too much pain to move, she was useless once again. Her position forced Romeo to shield her from behind. Take the brunt of more of those mysterious attacks.

While Velvet was so close by, yet too focused on dodging all those bolts the other wolf man was flinging back at her.

Was Romeo right?

They needed a strategy. Some tactics to save them form this disaster. And Juliet ... since she couldn't fight much, especially like this, but yet ...

Gulp.

Time to prove her worth.

Without even using her blade.

CHAPTER 36

ROMEO

Romeo crouched ready for the next punch that blond Bellon bastard would fling at him.

The moss beneath their feet should make one of them slip sooner rather than later, but if Romeo didn't hurry and come up with a better technique, or better strategy, or even better tactics ...

The murk around them was already getting chalkier and chalkier. The cloud of dust was rising. Surrounding them.

Burning his eyes.

Blurring his vision.

Just the taste of it ... his mouth was already so dry that ... that ... ugh, he needed a drink and soon. He could fight only so long without any food or drink, and he hadn't had anything all day.

Bellon laughed again.

"Ready for round 2?"

Then Dendre laughed right below.

"Born ready. Time for some clawgirl chow. I've always wanted a taste of you Velvet, and now, thanks to our masters, and your pathetic rebellion, I'll get to savor your flesh and bones as much as I always wanted!"

Velvet just sighed. Confident and scornful.

"How flattering. Your taste was always on the poor side. Both of you."

Both wolf man laughed this time, but Bellon answered first.

"You underestimate your taste."

Then Dendre chuckled. Loudly licking his chops too.

"And overestimate everything else about you."

Uh huh, but Romeo didn't make a sound—yet. Even if his heart pounded fast. Rhythm of battle fast. His sweat cooled him off with a few chills to boost.

So Romeo smirked at Bellon.

Smirked wide and haughty.

Haughtier than either of them.

"Right back at you—except for the taste. That's awful too."

And Romeo flung a Slash-o-Boom down.

Right at Dendre.

Whose gasp.

Attempt to dodge—almost failed.

Half his body was ruined. Destroyed.

But not his heart.

He regenerated far too quickly.

Just as Bellon bellowed.

Flung another flying punch at Romeo.

But Romeo let his feet dance. Dance right into a Spinning Bash.

Connecting with the flying punch.

Deflecting it downward.

So quickly.

But Dendre dodged even quicker.

The flying punch pounded into rock rubble.

Bounced back from the impact.

And smashed right through Bellon's broad chest.

But missed his heart. Again.

His regeneration kicking in far too fast.

Romeo would tired out long before either wolf man did.

When a roar from that dragon—from Juliet's father—shook the whole entire forest to its core.

CHAPTER 37

ROMEO

The dragon's roar even shook the very tree Romeo was standing on.

Shook it so fiercely that the moss nearly made him slip like Juliet had, but Romeo refused to go down like that. He had dwarf blood in him.

Time to prove how good that dwarf blood was.

Since right by the next tree, pressed sideways against its wide trunk, was that lousy dragon again. Still with Vueve, Fleur, and Claudia on his back.

And that huge bearded oak was already tilted badly. All from the dragon pressing hard against its trunk.

Those loud awful creaks said it all.

With a single flap of the dragon's wings, the cloud of dust was blasted away. Restoring Romeo's ability to see clearly. His eyes were no longer blurred or burning.

Except marched toward the dragon ... toward its side ...

Impossible.

But his eyes ... they couldn't be lying.

No.

A dragotroll?!

Yeah. A captain of terror among the baelzog's minions. This captain of terror was towering high and huge brute of green-scaled brawn in dark plate armor. Just that face ... a cross between deformed man-thing and dragon.

Just like how they were illustrated in the dime dreadfuls.

Even the smell ... thick awful serpent. More serpenty than the dragon even.

And this dragotroll held a massive iron club. A skeletal themed one. Along with a skull-themed broadsword across his back.

The dragon snarled at the dragotroll.

"Macker! You bastard! Don't you—"

A boom rang out.

That dragotroll Macker had already swung his club?

The dragon had already smashed the tree trunk?

Shaking the entire whole tree. Cracking its trunk.

Making it shower moss, leaves, and twigs.

And out fell a pink-haired blue-eared bunny beauty? In a shoddy red minidress. From high, high up.

And unseen by anyone else.

So far.

The dragon blasted flame at the dragotroll. That Macker thing. A blast utterly shrugged off by the dragotroll.

Then—wow. Macker swallowed up the flame.

Like … like … how a drunk would wish they could drink up a keg broken open and all the ale splashed out.

The pink-haired blue-eared bunny beauty landed right beside Fleur and Claudia. On her feet. So graceful. Outright catlike. And yet so quietly neither Fleur or Claudia noticed her—yet.

All Fleur, Claudia and Vueve were focused on Macker.

Just as Macker spat out a fireball.

Boom!

The fireball smashed into the dragon's head.

Staggering the dragon.

Wobbling the girls on his back dangerously.

Except for the bunny beauty. She moved with the wobble so well … then, with a maniacal grin she suddenly grabbed the heads of Fleur and Claudia, and …

!

They got sucked into her hands?!

In less the an instant. So quickly … that bitch!

And the pink-haired blue-eared bunny bitchy gained blonde highlights just as her shoddy minidress exploded. Replaced with a full clawgirl outfit. A suggestively-snug blue-themed leotard with bracers and thigh boots. Even a pair of pale blue scimitars were now strapped to her slim waist.

"Traitors," Masker said, "will suffer a fate worse than mere death."

The maniacal pink-haired blue-eared bunny bitch now was stalking up to Vueve when—

Juliet screamed, "DAD!"

And shifted into her clawgirl form.

Her peachy skin shifted to brilliant pink and protective scales. Hands and feet into eagle-style talons with bright ruby red claws.

Hand that couldn't hold her scimitar anymore. But right as she dropped it, Romeo grabbed it, and quickly.

Ready to hold back both Bellon and Dendre. Protect her to his fullest.

But the dragon snarled.

"Stay back, Juliet!"

Just as the maniacal bunny bitch absorbed Vueve. Gaining a pair of red locks to frame her awfully gorgeous face **and** a pair of similar swallowtail butterfly wings.

And yet the dragon was still completely unaware of the monstrous bunny bitch on his back.

But Juliet was already reacting. Her talons, her claws shot out, more like flung out, pink lightning bursting with ruby flames.

Lightning and flame that cracked and exploded against the ground, the ferns, the wood, as it charged toward Macker and the bunny bitch.

Flame Macker tried to smack aside with his club.

But the lightning shot through the club. His armor. Lighting it full of ruby flames.

Giving the dragon a moment to recover.

Dash toward Juliet.

Just as Macker swallowed the ruby flames.

Dashing faster and faster the dragon lifted off the ground. The bunny bitch still on top.

Until he rolled midair. Tossing her off. Hard.

Crashing into the ground.

While the dragon grabbed Juliet, Romeo, and Velvet with his talons safely.

Just as a crackling blast shot out at them.

From Macker.

A blast that smashed into the tree.

Destroyed it utterly.

Yet Romeo glimpsed the unthinkable. Bellon and Dendre both survived. By dodging last moment.

But so did the dragon.

Flying higher and higher.

Further and further away.

But not out of danger—yet.

CHAPTER 38

KROTHA RIGOT

Krotha was finally back in Shadow Forest. The murk was lighter than she remembered. Much lighter. The filthy earth and ground was musty than she recalled. So musty it drier out her skin and tentacles.

But now, as she was settled on top of this wolf man, on his head, those wretched ferns were mere fodder to be crushed. No longer a nuisance like they were on that wretched fox.

And this wolf man could carry both blades easily. No more need to waste any magical energy carrying them in less obvious but more convenient fashions.

Her own army of tendrils had been expanded to include delicious demihumans that that dragotroll Macker had killed only to raise them with her spore.

Make an army under her command, not his.

An army that heard every word that he and that last of

the baelzog had schemed. That the last baelzog retrieved two of the traitors, fused them together into a more potent clawgirl demibunny hybrid ... and would do that to the rest of those traitors.

Perfect for that tournament.

And a useful delay. For now.

To trap for her prey.

Her rivals. Since that baelzog would no doubt try to absorb Juliet. The clawgirl sacrifice needed to being the age of the hobgobble and end the age of mankind.

Her army all by itself was now ready suited to massacre mankind along with her rivals—all except for that one wretched boy she needed to capture and sacrifice just right. But against that Romeo boy an army of undead was ... less than useful.

She needed something more. More than just that traitor clawgirl Juliet as a hostage. More than his curved magical blade.

Something only a necromancer with such an amazing demon core could accomplish.

And what an accomplishment it would soon be.

Good thing she spared the fox with her spore in it.

Since it soon would be key to her ultimate victory.

But first she had to slow down that dragon.

No. Kill it.

But only once it got her prey close enough to that tournament.

CHAPTER 39

ROMEO

This time Romeo wasn't about to even think of any complaint about being caught like a rabbit in an eagle's claws, with him the rabbit and the dragon the eagle.

Of course, they were all soaring so high above Shadow Forest the forest itself was like a vast expanse of furry green carpet. Craggy mountains looming far in the distance.

And no so far distance.

Just the air by now was a chilly reminder of their crazy high height. How he failed to save both Fleur and Claudia from that bunny bitch. Failed Vueve too.

Despite holding both of Juliet's scimitars. Good swords. Good enough for most of his techniques—except maybe the Counter Kill one.

Maybe.

He mustn't fail Juliet, or Velvet.

Not again. Never.

But Vivian and Azura ... his heart sank at the obvious implication of what he saw back there.

That Vivian and Azura had already been absorbed by that ... *thing*.

The vast darkness roiling underneath the thick canopy of mottled green, of thick musty earth and all those unearthy screams and howls now ... no.

That bunny thing he would defeat. He had to, and quickly. Somehow rescue them all. But without a true magical blade. These human-bone scimitars were only so good ... and he couldn't use them in that tournament. No without lots of explaining.

Too much explaining.

(Probably.)

But he'd win that tournament. Win the ability to save his girls.

Velvet and Juliet wouldn't be the only two girls to survive. Not after all they went through.

Everything they survived together. Their whole future was ahead of them.

Cut short—unless he won that tournament.

And saved them quickly.

Before whatever that bunny bitch monster had done couldn't be undone and—

Another scream erupted. Shrill. Loud. And beyond inhuman.

Ahead of them. Well ahead of them.

Another giant green worm. With two pairs of giant slimy wings.

The dragon barked out scornfully.

"This coward again?"

He dove right at the giant worm.

But this time ... the worm charged back at them?

Straight at them.

Fearlessly.

The dragon laughed again.

"So some courage this time?"

So obviously, the crazy dragon blasted out some flame. A wall of roiling flame. Flame so hot it heated up everything. Even the very air they were crashing through.

Even as the flame turned to thick dark roiling smoke.

A wall of dark gray. Billowing horror.

That the dragon was flying straight toward.

Then veered into a sudden spiral.

Still toward the wall of smoke.

Just as the worm broke through the wall.

Straight through.

While the dragon spiraled around the worm.

Slashed its wings with his back spines.

Deep and hard.

While the dragon then swooped down, swung and flew right along the canopy.

All while the worm screamed. And so loud, in such pain Romeo couldn't hear himself think.

But no crash came from the canopy.

The worm hadn't dropped from the sky.

Not yet.

The worm had recovered. Had already turned. Dove down at them.

Juliet screamed.

"Its wings recovered?! Already?!"

Romeo gasped.

"Yeah. How ..."

Its huge maw was open. Closing in faster and faster. About to swallow them all up.

Velvet fired a shower of violet bolts down into the open maw. Filling the inner mouth with bits of violet bolts.

Bolts that sank into the mouth and vanished.

"Its too big," Velvet said, "My power won't take effect in time."

Juliet gagged.

"That stench ... I think it's more than that."

She was right. That stench was worse than swamp stench hell. The kind of stench only the crudest of patrons, always guys bragged about, often to Romeo, and on the side.

The dragon growled, and struggled to fly faster and faster, but ...

"I can't fly any faster. To think I'd struggle against that coward ..."

Romeo huffed.

"My Slash-o-Boom won't do much, but it might slow it down if I hit it enough times."

Juliet cried out, "No! Wait. I have on last idea ... just wait for it ..."

Romeo gasped. Scimitars ready.

"Huh? Tell me or else—"

"Wait means wait," Juliet said, "Didn't your uncle always say something ... what was it ..."

Trust his nose? Wait that ... that stench. So stronger. Stronger than last time too. Far stronger. Too strong.

What did it mean?

That maw was closer and closer.

Too close.

No any time left.

Its maw was over them. Sawteeth ringed around the maw. Razor sharp and slimy everywhere. Stinking of death and worse.

A moment from snapping shut.

And an instant before ending them all awfully terribly.

Juliet shouted.

"Now! Puri-pervert it!"

Ah! Of course!

Romeo unleashed a Puributcher. Right down its throat.

Flying through undead flesh. Then disintegrating it. Into a massive escape hole.

A hole that the dragon flew through by slowing down. Right as the maw snapped shut.

And then disintegrated.

The dragon barked a laugh.

"That's my girl!"

Juliet giggled so clearly happy, but the dragon went on and on.

"To think that basted went undead! Needing to die before gaining any—AAAAHHHH!"

Suddenly the dragon wobbled. The smell of blood and flesh ... his wing!

The dragon fell.

Tumbling through the canopy.

And Romeo knew no more.

CHAPTER 40
JULIET

Juliet didn't know what was more shocking: how hard that crash into the ground was or how sturdy she somehow was in her clawgirl form.

She gagged clumps of dirt and fern out of her mouth, and yet didn't cough out one bit of blood, or bits of her own fangs—as achy as they were—no, her tongue even checked. Carefully.

All her teeth were even fine.

Perfectly fine.

Just like her head. It was a bit woozy but nothing more. Even her hair. Long golden and not a single split end. Or too messy. Or tangled.

She sighed. Steadying herself. The musty earth was more than biting enough to clear away that wobbly wooziness in her head.

Clear up her confusion.

But she still trembled, half up, half lying on her side, her leotard was somehow intact too. Letting the wet soil soak through cold and jabbing.

But not a single rip?

Or scratch?

Ack!

A huuuuge wide tree trunk was right ahead of her. Its gnarled roots were woven thick and craggy around the rocky soil. Like a booby trap for … for … ugh.

Had she gotten flung any further … she'd be a splat on that mossy trunk.

Shutter.

No roars from dad? Nothing. That she dropped here and not … not … she couldn't even smell him and wow, was he smelly.

No sign of Romeo or Velvet either.

Gulp.

Was she alone? Again?

The murk was denser than her dad and Romeo combined, and there was no sign the canopy was damaged.

Not nearby. The murk was thicker the further away she looked. And her vision wasn't that bad. No. It was better than Romeo since he was only human and he kept saying just how murky and dark this place was.

Forcing herself to her feet, claws, talons whatever … Juliet almost called out for dad. For Romeo. For anyone but … no.

It was too silent.

Creepy silent.

No. A deep breath.

Just musty earthy icky that this whole entire forest tasted and smelled like but ...

She leapt up. Quickly. Onto the nearest branch. Like some terrified grasshopper.

Spooked grasshopper.

No. That cringe in her spine.

This wasn't enough

She leapt up higher.

And higher.

Then kneeled. Crouched low. Thick clumps of leaves surrounded her. All around her. The murk hid her despite her bright blue leotard. Her brilliant pink scales and ruby-red claws.

Claws she could at least defend herself with.

Mostly.

Sort of.

A rolling growl erupted nearby.

Behind her. No.

On the branch right above her?

On the thick branch shadowing this slimmer one.

Gulp.

Did she leap right into a trap?

Already?!

Another rolling growl erupted nearby. On a branch across from her.

Juliet didn't dare move.

She glanced its way.

Only glanced.

And nearly screamed.

CHAPTER 41

ROMEO

Romeo woke up utterly shocked he was still alive and (mostly) well. He had taken a big fall, maybe broken something, so, just like pa trained him, he wiggled his digits to check if any limbs were broken.

So wiggling his (bare?) toes and besides some aches ... his legs weren't broken. Good. Not injured too badly. He wiggled his fingers and yup, his arms still worked. No serious injuries there.

His whole entire body ached like he was tenderized by Aunt Tilda preparing a tenderloin for the patrons. Each breath ached, but mildly, so no broken ribs or worse.

The musty dank nipped his insides like the tiny annoying dogs some patrons loved to take everywhere with them. It all made him want to moan and vent his aches out into the world. But the silence around him, ugh, but he could hear himself breath, hear his heart beat, but not as the rhythm of battle.

Not yet.

Romeo took another deep breath. Calm deep breath just like pa taught him to. He was on his side. Slumped over a lump of dank soggy soil. Soil tickling his bare side. In a pile of ferns, rocks, and ... wait.

Where were Juliet's scimitars?

His hands ... were empty.

But he had them before he fell. He must have lost when he fell.

Maybe for the best. Good chance he would have skewered himself during the fall if he held onto them.

Still, hopefully they would return to Juliet magically, somehow, but better go look for them, and quickly. They were really, really needed, and soon.

So Romeo sat up.

Grunted.

Rock jabbed his ass through his slacks. Ferns slapped his bare shoulders and his chest was scrapped full of ruined fern.

But that whiff of almond and vanilla musk. From a gentle breeze right into his face.

That moan nearby. From a velvety girlie voice.

A familiar voice.

"Velvet?" Romeo said. "You alright?"

Another groan.

But a couple few paces ahead of him ... Velvet shoved herself up.

"Yeah, but I ..."

Her heart of. a baby face, her beautiful skin ... brilliant violet scales. Her hands were dark purple talons with black claws. Her long lush black hair covered her more than ... than ... oh no.

"My puributcher got you too ..." Romeo said, "Sorry, I—"

"No worries. Better alive and nude than dead and clothed, I always say."

Her black lips even smiled weakly at him.

But with another weak gasp, her heart of a baby face slumped. Framed messy yet beautifully by her long lush black hair. Hair that also ... her chest ... would be bare underneath ...

Romeo gulped.

"Velvet!"

He leapt up. With a yelp. From sharp aches from his whole entire body.

And he stumbled over to Velvet.

Collapsed to his knees before her. Too weak to stand up again.

Especially when she swept her long black hair behind her and gave him a tender but tired hug, and giggled out a smirk.

"Now it's our turn," Velvet said, "I'll need you to undo those pants. My talons aren't good for that kind of tender work, you see."

"Good point," Romeo said, "More like six good points."

She gave him a warm moany kiss. Pressed her ample buxom big chest against his pecks—a dream come true— especially with that sultry moan, as she rubbed them against him more and more.

Romeo didn't hesitate. His heart raced for more and more.

Made him tremble for more and more. His hands tingled for that blissful pleasure. Slid down her lush sides as she purred like a feline about to lap up catnip-flavored milk. Sleek and warm bliss down to her bare hips for more moaning pleasure that their kisses grew even more passionate.

The down to her bare sleek thighs.

More kisses.

More moans.

More trembling. Both of them. In pure joy finally being expressed.

He couldn't hold himself back any longer.

Romeo shoved himself out of his slacks. Flung them aside.

Just as Velvet pulled him down. Mounted him. Like he was the blade and she was the sheath. Pumping and pumping, moaning and moaning. She pulled his hands against her ample buxom big breasts.

Gasping for more and more.

Even when he seed erupted into her. More and more.

Even when she shrieked in joy.

And collapsed beside him.

Panting his name in his ear.

And embracing him from his side.

CHAPTER 42
JULIET

Juliet caught sight of the nightmare for only an instant, but an instant was all she needed to nearly scream her lungs out.

Thankfully the thick clumps of leaves blocked most of it from view. The murk was even thicker here, despite being closer to the bright blazing sun above the canopy.

There still was no sign of any damage to the canopy. Through where anyone fell through.

The light but harsh rustling of the leaves in the cold breeze froze her even more.

Serpent-still frozen.

The kind of freeze she could never do at the Honey Heart Resort. Or at the village nearby. Her life depended on not doing it.

But here ... out in the wilderness ...

To her side, crouching on that craggy thick branch next to

hers, was a powerful feline body, shaped and sized kinda like a cougar but with thick gray scales and six powerful legs instead of four. The kind of nightmarish creature Romeo would love to slay.

Even its talons, ick, it's like they belonged more to some horrifying bug-thing than a cat-thing.

She couldn't see its face.

But then ... maybe it couldn't see her, right?

Hopefully.

Another rolling growl broke out. Ahead of her. Not on this branch, but close.

Very, very close.

Taking a deep quiet breath ... the stink of bug, lizard, and cat combined? Weird, but the monsters of Shadow Forest were all weird horrors. Nothing normal here. Nothing at all.

Gulp.

Her hips ... felt a sudden extra weight? Wait. Her blades?! They were back in their sheaths!

Good, but ... Romeo would be defenseless now. She needed to find him. Before any of these horrors found him first.

But ... she didn't stand a chance against several cat-big-lizard horrors. Not with her skills.

So what were they waiting for? Did they not really know where she was? Did they even sense her near—

A shriek?!

A girl's shriek! Close by. Below.

Seven cat-thing gasps around her?

Seven?!

The girl shrieked again and wait, that kind of shriek, it wasn't out of fear or horror, but … those loud moans were full of pleasure not … not …

Juliet nearby growled herself, but the idea of finding Velvet and Romeo together and safe, even if they were having sex, better than either of them being dead, or lost.

A gust of wind.

The tree branch shivered. Nearby branches shivered. Creaked quietly.

And the cat-things were gone.

Gone after Romeo and Velvet.

No!

Not when they were so close. So close to escaping. Getting to that tournament. Getting to safety.

(Sort of.)

As safe as human places could be for a secret clawgirl.

Juliet whipped out her scimitars.

No. Tried.

But her talons—wait her talons!

No need for her scimitars right now.

She dashed out of her hiding spot.

The cat-things had already vanished into the murk ahead.

But not for long.

Juliet went grasshopper girl right there and then. Dashing, hopping branch to branch.

Hurrying over to the shriek and moans.

She caught sight of Velvet, Bare-in the scale and mounted above Romeo, who was lying on the ground.

Both utterly oblivious to the dangerous cat-things coming their way.

Cat-thing up on the branches above them.

Ready to pouch and kill them both.

Until Juliet flung a load of pink lightning with its ruby flames at the cat-things.

Exploding at least a couple of the nightmares.

Nightmares that turned toward her now.

With faces that ... Juliet screamed.

Those faces—like huge monstrous icky wasp-spider faces!

She flung wave after wave of lightning and flame their way. Blowing away more and more branches and monster cat-thing until—ack!

Hugged from behind? A warm comforting hug. That smell of almond and vanilla too ...

Velvet whispered into her ear.

"Thanks," Velvet said, "But they're gone now. You can calm down."

Juliet gulped.

Nodded.

"You ... you ... you're both alright? Right?"

Velvet giggled.

"More than alright. You want some Romeo time while I stand watch?"

"I ..."

But then Juliet saw a glint of something almost as good as Romeo time ...

And perfect for the coming tournament.

CHAPTER 43
ROMEO

Romeo still couldn't believe, after all they've been through together, just how great Juliet's vision was, how great clawgirl vision was in general.

Even from waaaaaaay up on the tall bearded oak, Juliet had been able to spot her precious chubby heart-shaped pouch, *despite* it being dropped many days ago and now hidden well underneath a clump of thick coiled ferns. That she spotted a glint of golden coin, from some spilled coins. Coins as golden as her hair, and this find, or more like recovery, would save them all lots of trouble if there were fees for the tournament.

Expenses only some quick coin could cover.

That the pouch, and its heavy load of coins were still safe and sound, despite having laid out here for days and days, in the middle of nowhere ... in the middle of Shadow Forest ... then again, that might have been why it was safe and sound.

Pretty much no one came this way, other than monsters.

And those monsters didn't care for gold. Only for flesh.

Then again, Juliet mentioned a bunch of protective spells were woven into it. Maybe those spells helped out after all too.

Romeo knew better than to fetch the pouch for Juliet. He merely stood near it. Waiting for Juliet to come and claim her precious pouch and all its coin once again.

That she saved him and Velvet from some kind of cat-monster pack by utterly savaging the cat-things and the branches above where he and Velvet ... gulp.

Did she really not like that Velvet and him were ... maybe not. Or at least she didn't want to show it. Not here anyway.

And now the discovery of her pouch with all its coin? It lit up face up so excited and joyful ... no doubt she had forgiven them all right there and then. She would have never found it if Romeo and Velvet hadn't ... you know, so of course Juliet forgave them all.

Juliet even went grasshopper girl and hopped down branch to branch, and her giggles and cheer was so intoxicating that Romeo couldn't help but grin wide himself at her.

The moment she landed near him she dashed right for her pouch.

Snatched it like it was the most precious thing in her life that instant.

Fixed it back on, off the side of her lopsided belt.

Then gasped. Looked at him guilty pouty.

"I ... you okay?"

"Yup. You?"

"Lots better now." Juliet giggled, and fondled her precious pouch. "We better hurry. Or else my dad's ... we need to get to the tournament, and quickly, but ..."

Romeo grimaced.

"Not dressed like that, we're not. That outfit just screams clawgirl."

Juliet gulped, nodded.

"But what else ..."

"I know. Since your pouch was here then—"

"I'm not lending you *any* coin—yet."

Okay, he should have expected *that* reaction.

"Not asking you to. The burlap bag with the weekly supplies, it must be around here somewhere. Close by."

"Ooo, good idea! That would definitely have some spare outfits in it. And that clearing can't be far."

Juliet already grabbed Romeo and soon, they were back in the tree tops.

Velvet not far behind.

CHAPTER 44

ROMEO

Amazingly enough, the burlap sack was almost right where Romeo left it.

Almost.

Now it was on the ground, not high up and safe in the bearded oak. It now laid right in front of the bearded oak with the wide crack Juliet once hid in to escape Romeo and then got attacked by jumping raptors.

That nothing had ripped open the bag and ruined what was inside ... strange.

Pa and Uncle Jethron, even Aunt Tilda, all had drilled into him how big nasties would go after a big sack with supplies if left on the ground, but hang it up high and far fewer nasties would go after it.

Usually.

And some big nasties clearly went after it anyway. The thick moss along the wide trunk was now bruised and scratched, but the damage was from days ago. The moss smelled rich but not freshly ripped.

So the last attempt was days ago.

Not recently, yet the bag seemed to have fallen recently. Judging by the way the leaves and twigs were freshly broken underneath it.

The way the moss was crapped underneath.

Fresh and smelly.

The clearing itself was brighter than the usual murk of Shadow Forest. A round clearing full of boulders jutting out of the dark dank soil. Plenty of grass poked through. Plenty of moss made the boulders themselves even more slippery.

And lost of tracks. Tracks of creatures Romeo didn't recognize.

Often tracks far bigger than his own feet.

Than even a clawgirl's taloned feet.

No doubt they would have gone after the burlap sack if it had been here a while. But the tracks were old. Softened. As dry and dark as the rest of the soil. With plenty of fallen leaves and twigs everywhere.

But no fishy stench of hobgobble. No sign of the jumping raptor's corpses either. Whatever wandered these woods already feasted on that meal days ago and left nothing behind.

When suddenly Romeo smelled that familiar rosy fragrance. Strong and sweet and so, so heart-thumping familiar that ... gulp.

"Vivian?" Romeo said.

More like whispered. Despite Juliet being right beside him.

And now, sniff, sniff—that cool breeze, and a hint of familiar bunny girl too?

"Azura ..." he said.

Gulped again.

Juliet even tensed beside him. Not saying a word.

Yet.

Except his hackles ... ack! They screamed danger *painfully* very, very suddenly.

A hunch.

Instinct.

Romeo grabbed Juliet. Sid-hugging her.

But it was Velvet that shoved them both out of the way.

Quickly.

"Look out!"

BBBOOOOOMMMMM!!!!

A familiar huge hammer smashed into the ground. Cratering right where Romeo and Juliet had been standing.

A massive crater.

But no damage to the burlap sack—yet?

Holding onto that huge hammer was that pink-haired blue-eared bunny girl.

The one who absorbed all the other girls.

In the same flimsy red minidress. And now with a savage looking blade strapped to her back.

She smirked at them all menacingly.

"Only three left? And you were all so tasty good!"

A flurry of violet bolts flew her way. From Velvet.

All deflected by that huge hammer. The clanks echoing loud and sharp. As sharp any as blade.

"Yum! Yum! I've always wanted to taste you, Velvet. You were one of my better creations too—until you betrayed us."

The bunny girl moved so fast Romeo hardly blinked and she was on Velvet.

Velvet screamed. "Run you idiots!"

She loosed another flurry of bolts at the bunny girl.

All deflected.

But slowing the bunny girl down. Some.

Juliet shoved her scimitars into Romeo's hands.

"We can't ... not Velvet too!"

Romeo gasped.

"You knew?"

Juliet nodded.

"I saw ... just hurry! I'll ... I'll ..."

"Behind me. Both of you!"

But for Velvet, it was too late.

Her scimitar bow held back the hammer.

Barely.

But not the follow up—a solid kick to her gut. A kick that absorbed her quickly into the bunny girl.

Romeo screamed.

"NNNNOOOOOOOO!!!!!"

Lunged.

Slashing at the bunny bitch.

Made contact—but no damage?!

Just passed through her. As if she wasn't even there.

The bunny bitch cackled.

"My own weapons cannot harm me you fool!"

And she swung the hammer again. To the side. Into his blades. Into him.

Smashing him aside.

Sending him flying.

High and helpless.

CHAPTER 45
JULIET

Juliet stood shocked and horrified at the sight of Romeo flying sideways through fern and murk away and further away.

And her helpless to help.

The clangs of her scimitars against that big huge hammer echoed sharp like knives stabbing the ears. Echoed even sharper around the murk at the edges of the clearing. Against the boulder jutting out of the ground.

The cackles of that bunny girl jabbed Juliet into action.

As unarmed as Juliet was ... there still were a few paces between her and that bunny girl. All because Velvet sacrificed herself. Had shoved Juliet and Romeo out of the way just in time.

The crater behind the bunny girl a testament to that girl's deadly strange strength. The very smell of crushed vaporized rock and earthy dust almost made Juliet gag.

Slow down a touch.

But no.

If she lost this time, then that awful prince long ago, the one she let win despite her ability to beat him back at the Honey Heart Resort, that he realized it and called her dumb and worthless would actually be right.

Her scimitars were worthless against that bunny girl for some reason but what about her clawgirl powers?

Summoning all her fear, her rage, her fury at the loss of her pack, after the many years of being all alone and and and —GGGRRRRR!!!!

Juliet flung pink lightning at the bunny girl. Ruby red flame igniting wherever the lightning struck. Whether boulder, fern, or moss.

Yet the bunny girl slapped the lightning away with her hammer.

"Weren't you listening, stupid?" the bunny girl said. "There's nothing a clawgirl can do to harm me, your creator, Lady Gryllmore!"

Romeo was already up. Crawling among the ferns closer and closer, but behind the bunny girl, Lady Gryllmore.

So Juliet tsked. Pouted even fiercer.

"Lady who? Never heard of you."

That got a growl out of Gryllmore.

"You'll suffer for that, clawgirl. I choose you to be the greatest among your kind and you ... you spat in my—"

Juliet actually spat in Gryllmore's face.

The shocked surprise got that Gryllmore to freeze for an instant.

The instant Romeo needed to pounce on Gryllmore.

And snatch the blade off her back?

Gryllmore screamed. Swinging her hammer right at Romeo.

"Get your hands off me you disgusting—"

"Puributcher!"

Point-blank range. Smashing through Gryllmore.

And then Juliet.

Her outfit gone *again*.

But so was Gryllmore. Gone forever.

Along with her pack. Forever.

CHAPTER 46

KROTHA RIGOT

Krotha wailed in utter bliss and glee. She could feel it. Like a weight lifted off her entire being. Like a new coat of slime, tingling and fresh smelling.

Her last and final rival had passed from this world. No more baelzog to challenge her.

To interfere with the coming age of the hobgobble.

Or undeath.

Her tendrils were stationed near the boy and girl, Romeo and Juliet. Up high in those filthy reeking trees. Their spears ready to rain death but no, their deaths had to be by her own tentacles.

Least their final end.

Her tendrils, her army could only help tenderize the two, prepare them for their coming doom.

Through the murk and the destruction, that fool Gryll-more had carried the Savage Blade of Shadow Forest with her, on her back even, and it spelled her doom, as it would to any female foolish enough to try to carry that blade, use it, despite its arrogantly foolish nature.

Just like it led that other clawgirl to her doom.

No.

She mustn't handle that blade, but there was no need to either.

With three magical blades, that would be enough.

Riding solidly latched onto this wolf man's head, Krotha would reach the boy and girl soon enough. Her demonic core was more than ready for the coming fight. His techniques no use against Krotha herself, since both this wolf man and her were very much alive.

Her tentacles driven into the wolf man's brain, his mind, her spore not necessary this time.

No more need for that tournament anymore.

Their deaths were coming.

And nothing would save them now.

Nothing.

CHAPTER 47
ROMEO

Romeo and Juliet were as silent as the rest of Shadow Forest. His harem, her pack, gone, and they were once again alone together.

Least Juliet now had her scimitars back and Romeo had a magical blade. He could feel the power surging through his hand from the blade, like a rush of rapids, of adventure powering through his veins. The tingle of each and every of his hackles shot up and stayed up.

It hadn't spoken to him, like Vivian claimed it did to her, but no need to rush things.

The burlap sack was still untouched and unharmed. The new crater no real obstacle but it was a bit of trouble. The smell of vaporized dirt and boulder was already biting his insides, but now ...

"Juliet, do you ... or should I check for a change of ..."

Juliet gulped. Pecked his cheek.

"I will."

Romeo began to turn around, but Juliet tugged him back.

"No need to turn around."

She even giggled. Her smile as perverted as ... as ... well ...

"Watch if you want."

And Juliet strutted over to the burlap sack. Sorted through its contents and found a similar honey heart resort outfit that she had originally had on.

Of course, Aunt Tilda often had a couple of the same outfits in case one needed mending or more.

Slipping off her blue leotard, letting Romeo see her bare in the peaches and cream delightful skin, even if she covered her chest and crotch shyly right now, his cheeks blazed as much as Juliet's no doubt would have if she were human.

When a long thin shadow flickered high above her.

Sped down at her.

At her back.

A spear!

Romeo called out.

"Watch out! Above you!"

And he loosed his Slash-o-Boom Technique.

Destroying the spear.

No. Not just one spear.

Several spears?!

Juliet yelped.

Bare in the nude but she didn't hesitate this time.

She grabbed her scimitars. Snapped them into a bow.

Loosed a flurry of bolts into the canopy.
Booms and screams rang out.
The stink of rotting fish?!
"Hobgobbles!" Romeo and Juliet cried out together.

CHAPTER 48
ROMEO

There was no doubt about it. Up. In the bearded oak with the crack down its mossy trunk. Among the many thick twisting branches.

Within the murk.

The source of that rotting fish stink.

The sight of that rotting blueberry blue. Of tentacled hobgobbles.

All armed with spears.

Spears flung at both Romeo and Juliet. Throughout the whole entire clearing.

Romeo unleashed his Slash-o-Boom Technique on them all. Destroying branch after branch. Hobgobble after hobgobble.

Letting it rain shards of musty wood.

But more hobgobbles kept coming.

Appearing.

No.

Recovering? The damage he inflicted didn't last.

All the hobgobbles recovered just as quickly.

Juliet fired another flurry of bolts.

Exploding more hobgobble.

Yet they recovered just as quickly.

Juliet growled. Backing up to Romeo.

"They're all undead! Romeo, you know what to do!"

Romeo knew exactly what to do.

"Puributcher! Puributche1! Puributcher!"

So many hobgobble now crumbled away.

But more took their place?

Again, Romeo unleashed more puributchers.

More hobgobbles crumbled away to nothingness.

Yet more kept coming.

And more

And more.

Romeo grabbed Juliet and dashed to escape.

Spears savaging the ground behind them.

CHAPTER 49

ROMEO

Romeo dashed as fast as he could. All the while holding Juliet's hand. Both of them dashing for safety. Through ferns ripping at their legs. Leaves and twigs snapped beneath their feet.

To find another clearing.

A better place to fight back.

Away from the hobgobble horde in the canopy behind them.

A horde spearing the ground behind them full of spears. Like a pin cushion. Cutting through soil and boulder alike now.

Until the unthinkable blocked their way.

A snarling wolf man. Big. Dark. Brawny.

With a small but familiar hobgobble latched onto his head.

And two blades were in his hands. One an unfamiliar bastard sword. The other Romeo's familiar crescent blade.

His harpe.

Romeo attacked without hesitating.

"Puributcher!"

The attack passed through them both. No effect? The ferns around them only stirred slightly. The trees nearby creaking ever so slightly.

No.

Both enemies were alive and well then.

Then ...

Romeo cried out. Slashing out as powerful as he could.

"Slash-o-Boom!"

The wolf man circled his bastard blade.

"Whirlwind Shield!"

And that deflected the Slash-o-Boom Technique?

It smashed into a nearby tree. Destroying it. Revealing a clearing of grass ... and a canyon.

Ah! The canyon Romeo had been walking along when he first when this way.!

"Romeo!" Juliet cried out. "Behind us! No more time!"

Juliet shoved her scimitars into the ground and shifted back into her reptilian form.

"Together!"

Romeo attacked with his Slash-o-Boom.

Juliet with her pink lightning and ruby flame.

Together they cried.

""Slash-o-Shock!"

The wolf man cried out.

"Sunfire Shield!"

Block the whole entire attack.

No.

More than block.

Flung it back at Romeo and Juliet.

The hobgobble cried out.

"Now die so the age of the hobgobble can begin!"

But Romeo wasn't out of tricks yet.

Like a spring ready to be triggered. A technique that would have made both pa and gramps proud. Romeo used the Counter Kill Reversal Technique.

Perfectly too.

Reversing it. Right back at the wolf man.

But the wolf man was ready for that too?

"Sunfire Shield!"

And reflected the counterattack back.

But not at Romeo.

At Juliet.

The hobgobble cackled a horrible girlish scream.

Striking up another idea. A desperate last idea.

So Romeo screamed back.

"Spinning Slash Bash!"

Caught the counterattack.

Flung it back at the wolf man.

Along with his blade at the hobgobble.

Juliet cried out.

"Romeo, no!"

But Romeo tripped. Fell to his knees.

Hoping beyond hope his guess was right.

Just as the hobgobble caught the blade.

The wolf man let the attack rip him in half—and recover just as quickly.

The hobgobble raised the Savage Sword of Shadow Forest.

"Now let the age of the hobgobble begin!"

And cut down.

At Romeo.

Juliet screamed.

And lashed out at the same time.

The savage blade missed!

Missed by far.

While Juliet's lightning hit the hobgobble.

Ripping into it. Destroying the wolf man's head.

But the wolf man recovered quickly.

The hobgobble was flung back. Screaming.

Landed near the clearing.

A fox suddenly appeared underneath it?

Yes. A fox in utter agony. With green spore infesting its whole body. Its eyes gone. Its head a cruel mess. The hobgobble latched onto it.

But where did the fox come from?

The hobgobble screamed. Waved that Savage Sword at Romeo and Juliet.

"I'll be back! This is not over! I—ack!"

The fox dashed away.

Onto a rope bridge that ... that rope bridge?!

The mimic bridge ... smiled.

Just like the fox.

The bridge opened its planks in half. Like a giant mouth.

The hobgobble screamed.

"Go fox go! Go you stupid—AAAAAAHHHH!"

And it swallowed them both.

Moments later screams erupted behind them. Of undead hobgobbles returning to the death that had originally claimed them ... until no more enemies were there.

Except the wolf man.

A wolf man who bowed and thanked them?

CHAPTER 50

MACKER THE CRUEL

Macker the Cruel felt the agony, the fury of his Mistress as she passed from this world, as the last of their masters passed from this wretched world.

Macker fell to his knees. Digging them deep into he ground and wailed out the agony that the other fodder must soon follow, would soon feel.

He pounded the ground, pounded the rocks into the rubble that humanity would soon become, would soon—ack!

A razor sharp blade burned through his throat?

Impossible! He was immune to all flames to—

He gagged. The pain. The darkness.

Yet he ... he managed to looked up.

At some vixen demihuman that looks so tasty good and yet so familiar and yet so ...

"For my brothers," she snarled, "and all the others you killed for your stupid schemes."

And she wasn't alone?

Macker tried to curse them. Tried to rise and tame their rebellion.

But then a terrible pressure pounded into his back.

A hammer?

That scream of fury. A bunny girl and her hammer?!

And she wasn't alone.

Other demihumans crowded around him.

All growling furious.

And he was too weak to resist their bloodlust, their determined fury to send him to their former masters.

CHAPTER 51
ROMEO

Romeo was once again at the canyon he started his adventure at. A canyon a few good times wider than he was tall, but this time, there was no weird rope bridge to distract him.

Just the usual pathway of grass and soil.

His bare feet gripped the soft grass and soil. Stretched and wiggled. Savoring his newfound freedom and new beloved girlfriend Juliet.

The burlap sack was now backpacked against his back. A heavy sack, especially now with the added weight of her scimitars and clawgirl outfit deep within it.

But the real bridge was still hours away. The real road made a very wide curve around Shadow Forest, and a curve Romeo was thankful for shortcutting.

More like long cutting.

The memories of his prior harem ... no. Too soon.

Even the sky was a bit cloudy, but not rainy, not yet.

Plenty of time to celebrate their victory.

Their success.

Even with only a little more time to enjoy the cool crisp smell of the river below. Echoes of the splashes and foamy crashes against unyielding boulders. Slaps as loud as the kind Juliet once inflicted on him.

But no more.

No sign of trouble along the bearded oaks of the other side of the canyon. No more hobgobbles.

They were all gone now. Least in this area.

Just like most of the clawgirls in this region—except for Juliet.

Maybe even the demihumans, but who knew? Poor Azura was gone. Whether any other demihumans survived ... none of his business.

Sure, Aunt Tilda would be furious at how late Romeo and Juliet would be getting back.

Furious at her loss of so many of her honey heart girls.

So many patrons vanished too. All due to that hobgobble necromancer.

No doubt Aunt Tilda would be even more upset at their announcement to be married very, very soon.

Just the musty smell of the bearded oaks reminded him of his grand adventure for these last few days. An adventure of a lifetime, if not more.

Even Juliet and her scent now. Her peaches and cream delight with that hint of cherry.

Like a desert for the eyes and loins.

The best dessert ever.

She had already slipped on her new top. A bra top of blue heart cupping the biggest moneymaking breasts at all of Honey Heart Resort, well, even before, back when there was competition.

Her ass was finer than ... than ... gulp.

Brainfart.

Again.

Her miniskirt was now a pair of upside-down blue hearts strapped together with stretchy white silk. They provided just enough coverage that a patron would normally only need to undress her a little with their eyes.

Or, in his case, remember that lovely fine ass, since it left the side of her lush hips bare.

But he knew it would never show more than she let it. That magical pentacle woven on the underside of the hearts would ensure no free peeks—ever.

Her stiletto footwear would stab anyone who dared look too low and underneath.

Except for him now.

A view she clearly meant to let him see plenty of in the coming days.

This itself path wasn't commonly taken, so no sign of other travelers since Romeo and Juliet had come this way.

Thankfully. More time alone to enjoy each others company.

Except for the wolf man popping up again.

The wolf man had shifted back into a human form. He was actually some noble who worked for the king himself.

That long speech, so formal, and yet so promising.

Gather clawgirls and others willing to fight against the monster menace.

A menace Romeo and Juliet would soon help fight against too. A menace already fading due to their adventure in Shadow Forest.

But that was a tale for another time.

For now they were returning home, To Honey Heart Resort, and would arrange their future from there.

A good promising future together.

As husband and wife.

ABOUT THE AUTHOR

Widely traveled, Jonathan Evan Hudson spends as much time studying life as he does writing gripping tales of fantastic adventures. From the giant redwoods of California to the deserts of Israel, his thrilling stories all draw on first-hand experiences and expand them with the fantastic and his acclaimed creativity.

Be the first to know!
For the updates and more:
www.JonathanEvanHudson.com

youtube.com/@jonathanevanhudson
tiktok.com/@jonathan.evan.hudson

A War Of Lust And Oak

Read Now!

THE ELF GIRL EFFECT

READ NOW!

The acclaimed Jonathan Evan Hudson once again weaves an unforgettable tale brimming with spicy page-turning action and fast-burning enemies-to-lovers passion.

Meet the newly knighted Roo Vorshaya. Sworn to protect humanity in the isolated mountain town of Appleharth. Dreams of action-packed adventure and passionate love under a lovely but sinister strawberry-pink sky.

Love re-ignited by a whiff of the familiar peaches and cream scent of his long-lost childhood girlfriend: the notorious elven witch Amber Peaches.

And endangering everything Roo holds dear.

Love page-turner novels of epic fantasy? Love reading from dusk to dawn? Then go read *The Elf Girl Effect* now!

Martial Art Of The Phantom Saber

Read Now!

SUCCUBUS SLASH

The acclaimed Jonathan Evan Hudson weaves an unforgettable tale of thrilling action and adventure spiced with fast-burning romance and doused deep in epic fantasy.

Enter Miles Mayhem. Rich in friends and enemies. And a fat boy badass in the sword.

A seriously delicious smell of bacon and eggs smothered in spiced razor-hot cheddar signals celebration—and serious trouble ahead.

Trouble beyond anything Miles ever expected.

The perfect epic fantasy novel. A genre-enlarging feast for fans of sexy action and fabulous adventure. Read *Succubus Slash* now!

Sword Master Of Honey Heart Resort

Read Now!

Into Shadow Forest

Read Now!

A diamond in the rough the bestselling Jonathan Evan Hudson weaves a thrilling tale from explosive beginning to satisfying end in the awe-inspiring land of Grandcrest.

The talented twenty-something sword master Romeo Bladell yearns for love and adventure.

And at the musty edges of Shadow Forest. Near the towering high oaks bearded like stout old dwarves. By a canyon like a wound gnashed deep through in the granite. A canyon like the maw of a stone dragon.

A strange unexpected rope bridge hangs silently. Sinisterly.

Beckoning adventure—and danger unimaginable.

Enter *Into Shadow Forest* and savor the most spectacular of page-turning epic fantasy novels. Love unique monsters, riveting battles, and fantastic femme fatales? Then read *Into Shadow Forest* now!

Angels Of The Sword

Read Now!

CROSSING OF SHADOWED DEATH

READ NOW!

The acclaimed master of fantasy Jonathan Evan Hudson once again shines through with his talented story-telling. Time to enter another stunning awe-inspiring world of dangerous demons, magical mayhem, and action-packed adventure.

A simple demon-hunting mission. The young and lonely Dirk yearns for amazing adventure, for gorgeously under-dressed dancer girls among the towering high ferns. Among the even taller pines of the hot and humid Fern Shadow Forest.

Pine needles everywhere. And so fragrant they made the finest of teas.

Sturdy reliable cobble roads of the Divine Empire cut through the whole entire forest. Providing the only safe passage.

Or so Dirk thought ...

Enjoy this sexy, action-packed epic fantasy adventure from the talented Jonathan Evan Hudson. Love to read an enthralling epic fantasy novel full of stunning rip-roaring battles with creative new monsters? Then go read *Crossing of Shadowed Death* now!

A TASTE OF THE ELF GIRL EFFECT

The acclaimed Jonathan Evan Hudson once again weaves an unforgettable tale brimming with spicy page-turning action and fast-burning enemies-to-lovers passion.

Meet the newly knighted Roo Vorshaya. Sworn to protect humanity in the isolated mountain town of Appleharth. Dreams of action-packed adventure and passionate love under a lovely but sinister strawberry-pink sky.

Love re-ignited by a whiff of the familiar peaches and cream scent of his long-lost childhood girlfriend: the notorious elven witch Amber Peaches.

And endangering everything Roo holds dear.

*Love page-turner novels of epic fantasy? Love reading from dusk to dawn? Then go read **The Elf Girl Effect** now!*

CHAPTER I

The sky was a strawberry custard for the eyes, and the same color of the lips Roo yearned to kiss.

So what if the clouds behind him were dark and ominous? The wind gusty and chilled more than the perfect shot of vodka. The taste of rain electrified by lightning-to-be ...

The street was as slim as his chances of success.

The cobble as bumpy as the journey ahead.

And this hill — a steep ascent into danger.

Roo even wore a jerkin woven of the finest dragon scale the son of ~~an~~ thee Exiled Exorcist of Most Notable Notoriety could hope to earn as one of the last members of the Vorshaya Clan.

Yup.

The Vorshaya clan. The once very badassed clan nearly wiped out to protect the greatest of the great Oak of Ages, a

205

source of lightful magic and all from ... something, something he'd hunt down and deal with.

Still, if his mother hadn't been doing scholarly stuff far away at the time ... if she hadn't taken him with her ...

Sigh.

He didn't like to think about it much.

But his jerkin was pale blue as the sky ... wasn't today.

But it was one only worn by the best of the best True TriCross Knights. The big, white triple cross on his chest proclaimed it for all to see.

And a chance to pursue his dream to travel the world.

Slay monsters and save people, without any of that bounty hunter nonsense either.

Explores things, places that no one's ever explored before, or okay, more like no one's explored in living memory ...

Or longer.

His jerkin, it even had the snazziest, puffiest shoulder guards of the palest, bluest cold silver, and they were so so perfectly round that a certain Motherly Scholar of Notable Nagging couldn't hope to find a single fault with.

Just like the trusty pouch she made for him.

Shaped like a chubby triple cross, it was strapped to his waist and she magicked it to hold far more than you'd think it could and weigh so much less.

And just like his pouch, his slacks were as blue as the sky ... wasn't ... today.

And ... okay okay.

Anyways, his boots, and girls were obsessed with footwear or else the boot merchants wouldn't cater to girls so utterly much, so anyways, his boots were a snazzy dark blue suede, like the coming night sky should be (but obviously won't be. Pink sky meant severe storm coming.)

And with the coming storm ...

There were even spooky tentacles of mist rising from the street, and that only happened when a serious storm was coming through.

But the not so distant rumbles ... wasn't only thunder.

So not much time left ...

Good thing he wore a pair of sabers and a whip. One saber was of the bluest, sharpest cold silver, and the other, the blackest, sharpest cold steel, a stronger variant of cold iron, and the whip was made of pretty strong scarlet dragon scales, with the dragon magic woven strongly within the whip.

Good for offense and defense, against magical and nonmagical trouble too.

Sort of.

As long as he didn't whip his eye out, like his mother often teased.

Even more important, his trusty arm guards were both cold silver and cold steel forged together. His left arm guard could extend into a shield. The right held a miniature bow with a string of holy blue magic so that, with the right motion flicking motion, it would fire bolts of holy blue light or unholy violet light.

Perfect for a True TriCross Knight.

His heart raced for the coming battle.

For the girl she would soon save.

Since nothing, absolutely *nothing* raced a heart like that elven fragrance, that whiff of the sweetest of peaches and cream only moments ago in this sweet sweltering hot afternoon.

No doubt about it.

The elf girl of his wildest dream come true. Right now. Here in the sexy flesh ...

Amber Peaches: a lust dream come true.

No.

Thee one and **best** lust dream come true.

And the muddy road here was a nice reminder of years ago, back when Peaches and Row got to quipping each other and their quipping got so fierce it broke out into mud wrestling that if, today their reunion broke into mud wrestling, wow, that would be so sexy amazing ...

Sniiiiiiiff.

It smelled ... surprisingly fresh. Earthy forest mud, no, soil fresh.

The lampposts at the street corners ... they were cold iron. The blackest of cold iron and forged like incredibly narrow, but tall, tulips of utter moonless midnight black.

Ah.

The oil lamps on top were those genie-style lamps to be wicked for the evening and wow, did they make the olive oil merchants rich.

But ... it was the genies inside that kept the mud clean. Kept their lamps lit at night, but what those genies were ...

Elf girls captured and lamped into genies due to the war

between humans and demons, and well, elves were demons after all, and elves were the fully evolved form of fairies.

Even Peaches.

But the rumble of distant thunder that wasn't thunder was almost louder than his own tummy rumbling for some peaches and cream pie, especially after that sexy whiff of long missed Peaches.

(All better to tease Peaches with too.)

((Sure, elves should thank the Light their natural body odor, after lots of sweaty work, was so fruity nice rather than so gut-wrenching stinky like humans, you know, like him, but either way, frequenting the public baths, a necessity, human or elf.))

(But not first date material.)

((Outside of certain smut rags kept hidden under the best lock and key in an undisclosed location.))

(((*Very* undisclosed.)))

Even now, the sun was still as blonde as Peaches' waist-long hair, so no worries.

Last they ran into each other, back before war and puberty tore them apart, her hair was ass-long but also far far messier.

Just like back then, she styled the bangs to fountain off the sides of her head like gorgeously floppy wings, plus a floppy witch hat of rosy pink, that, of course, would hide her huuuuge but adorably pointy elf ears.

Ears so long and pointy, that resembled a cross between kitty and fawn ears, especially how they always were moving about so expressively.

So all in all, he wasn't so distracted by her fine ass in a finer minidress, (and it was the ultra-short, ultra snug and stretchy kind that was like strawberry custard to the eyes, ears, and loins,) so no, in that critical moment, he didn't walk into a wall.

No.

He walked into a door.

And as the Light would have it, there was plenty of wall he could of walked into.

The stone floors of the half-timber houses all along this block. All painted as colorfully as a field of wildflowers, but full of apples, apple blossoms, and even more apples.

This town was called Appleharth for a reason.

A very good reason.

And the door he did walk into was the usual solid sturdy oak, so no worries, it took the beating well.

Sure, there was … a crack down the middle of the door now.

Sure. From him.

But the door's paint job was still spectacular.

No clumsy clod could hope to ruin those artful swathes of banana streaks full of cherry swirls. In fact, there wasn't even a nick to show for his clumsy moment.

Other than a wide crack down the middle.

And by the hinges too.

Roo credited his snazzy cowl and mouth cloth for softening the blow. They were as pale blue as the sky … wasn't … today.

But they were the color of Peaches' bright blue eyes …

well, last time they ran into each other years and years ago, over a decade ago. More than a decade ago. Wait. Same thing. Okay.

Good.

Dazed but not confused. A door would not stop him.

Or delay him.

Much.

Now one more chance or else ... he'd regret it for the rest of his life.

CHAPTER 2

PEACHES

Totally fucking … that poster of parchment … those blocky black letters spelling WANTED …

Oh, for the Oak of Ages … Peaches totally fucking wanted to give the middle finger to that sly sneak of a trickster the moment she spotted that parchment poster hanging all cozy and sinister and sooo much like a little black widow on those shutters behind the windowsill of those stinkier than stinky roses.

The sky wouldn't be the only one growling soon.

Good thing Peaches wore her finger loop gloves snug and ready. Each was as scarlet red as she'd soon make that trickster, what's her face, the Rouge Reapist, and even better, there were pentacles of unicorn hair woven into each palm to speed up her magic casting faster than a fox pouncing a mouse.

Along the glove were cute heart-shaped gaps. Normally,

they'd hold rosy pink hearts, each of which held a precast spell she could fling at a target for instant effect, but she ran out a while ago and seeing a human alchemist … pretty dangerous when her kind made such good ingredients to those sorts.

But that thunder close by, not just thunder.

The narrow street echoed the rumble and only confirmed the groan of a dire ogre coming this way.

Strange how there weren't any screams.

Disturbing, in fact.

Regular people shouldn't be so calm around one, unless … no.

Peaches didn't want to think of it.

Yet.

It was bad enough that the pink sky, as lovely as it was, meant the coming storm would be terrible, if her father's stories held any truth to them.

(Big if.)

But no telling what these half-timber houses were hiding then. So what if they were beautifully decorated with apples, apples, and more apples? Plus a flower or two.

A chill seemed to ache her whole spine.

A warning of danger.

Demonic danger.

Nearby.

Never mind elves were technically lightspawn, a kind of demon, but of the light, so too many humans, sigh.

Least she usually could be reborn a few more times.

More than a few, actually.

Nine lives, like a cat, but three already used, but least her power and beauty were upped each time, but she started out as a brand new fairy, hatching from the Oak of Ages, and had to find another compatible human girl to fuse with, eat her soul and sigh.

No wonder some human despised demons of   all sorts.

If her brother only had one life … if she only had one life … like these humans … sigh.

Why Roo even understood way back when … sigh.

But the lamppost of black iron, horribly styled like tall and narrow tulips, no, that burn to their smell, a burn like that death pepper chili that little brat Roo tricked her stupid bratty self into trying long ago (and stupid her tried it again and again and again …)

But it was definitely cold iron.

A quick way to a really, really awful death.

No wonder she couldn't pinpoint the source of demonic danger.

No doubt it was darkspawn demons but so what?

This was just a step toward her true dream, becoming an elf witch explorer, and discover why there's so many ruins appearing here and there, and elves had extension records proving some of these ruins appeared without a civilization before, as if it had been moved there.

Some even came from the future.

Others were from the distant past. Ruins that should no longer exist.

Ruins full of monsters.

So today, good practice.

Peaches made a point to keep strutting down the road without hesitation or obvious concern.

If orcs were hunting her ... letting them know she sensed something suspicious, especially as a witch with her fore-sense able to detect danger and ill intent toward her, well, according to her training, a big no no.

And despite it being in the early afternoon, the shutters of all the half-timber houses were shut.

Locked.

Other human towns she'd been in ... plenty of dumb human girls overlooked her demonic side and drooled over her looks, but here, today? Nope. Not one dumbass to brush off.

Something was off.

Good thing she could summon her bow and arrows of light quicker than any other elf in her generation, guy or girl. Several split seconds ahead of the best of the best guys and rapid fire better too. She could even build up plenty of blessed arrows as long as she got enough sunlight during the day, each day to build up and store more blessings for arrows for when she'd need them.

At least if any orc managed to get too close, the stiletto heels of her thigh boots could double as slyly placed daggers.

Alicorn style. Beauty and power came together for elf girls, so lucky her.

And her alicorn was the high grade spiraled kind.

Her boots were as scarlet red as she'd made those orcs.

Normally, she had rosy pink hearts lacing them snug up

her leg. They normally would hold spells she could fling off for instant magical attacks just like her gloves.

But right now, like her gloves, they were just a bunch of heart-shaped gaps.

At least her rosy pink minidress and witch hat were woven with silk of a spellbinder silkworm. They weren't protective against blade and fang, or even against magic ... but they both together were a huge reserve of extra magic that naturally refilled as long as she wore them enough, especially in sunlight.

Even today.

And to fuck with the mind of those perverted orc bastards, she went with the sluttiest minidress she could manage. Translucent silk, so the right angles, the right nude elf deluxe, he-he.

So double the weirdness that no human guys went lusty dumbass toward her today.

Not even the gate guards.

Okay. Gate guards rarely did. Being a guard was all reputation and honor, not about coin. Any act tarnishing that, tarnished all the guards, and the guard loathed that.

Plus, her rosy pink minidress had the perfect distract and destroy notch down the front. One that showed far more than the little it covered.

Including her bra of ruby hearts.

And her chest, buxom to the extreme.

With only a few stretched to the breaking ruby ties down each the notches, the slutty side notches revealed more than just her tasty midriff, they revealed a good solid hint of her lace panties.

Ruby lace.

Orcs were rapeholic monsters, after all. She might as well use their lust smitten idiocy against them.

Roo would so laugh and approve.

(And leer.)

((Leer plenty.))

(((Sigh. *Boys.*)))

((((But if he didn't ... her pointy tipped boots, his rear, he-he.))))

WANT MORE?

Go to

WANT MORE?

Go to

www.JonathanEvanHudson.com